The Impossible Clue

Also by Sarah Rubin

SOMEDAY DANCER

The Impossible Clue

SARAH RUBIN

Chicken House

SCHOLASTIC INC. /

Cuyahoga Falls Library
Cuyahoga Falls, Ohio

Copyright © 2017 by Sarah Rubin

All rights reserved. Published by Chicken House, an imprint of Scholastic Inc., *Publishers since 1920*. SCHOLASTIC, CHICKEN HOUSE, and associated logos are trademarks and/or registered trademarks of Scholastic Inc.

First published in the United Kingdom in 2016 as *Alice Jones: The Impossible Clue* by Chicken House, 2 Palmer Street, Frome, Somerset BA11 1DS. The publisher does not have any control over and does not assume any responsibility for author or third-party websites or their content.

No part of this publication may be reproduced, stored in a retrieval system, or transmitted in any form or by any means, electronic, mechanical, photocopying, recording, or otherwise, without written permission of the publisher. For information regarding permission, write to Scholastic Inc., Attention: Permissions Department, 557 Broadway, New York, NY 10012.

This book is a work of fiction. Names, characters, places, and incidents are either the product of the author's imagination or are used fictitiously, and any resemblance to actual persons, living or dead, business establishments, events, or locales is entirely coincidental.

Library of Congress Cataloging-in-Publication Data available

ISBN 978-0-545-94025-2

10 9 8 7 6 5 4 3 2 1   17 18 19 20 21

Printed in the U.S.A. 23

First edition, January 2017

Book design by Abby Dening

For Henry and Matilda

250

(1

I WAS TRYING to prove Goldbach's Conjecture, but I wasn't getting very far. Maybe it was the fact that it hadn't been cracked by some of the greatest mathematical brains in history. Then again, maybe it was the steady stream of spitballs hitting the side of my head that was stopping me.

"Do you mind?" I turned in my seat and glared across the aisle.

Kevin Jordan smiled, the straw still clenched in the side of his mouth. "What?" he asked, raising his eyebrows.

"You know what."

"No I don't."

I knew I should have stayed in bed that morning. Kevin Jordan had a face like one of those angels Michelangelo painted in the Sistine Chapel. He had the personality of a fungal rash.

I took a breath and counted up in prime numbers until the urge to throw my pencil at his face subsided. I got to 101.

Mrs. Wright had moved Kevin to the desk next to mine because I was supposed to be a good influence. Like my smart would rub off on him. Unfortunately, Kevin had spent the entire year making it his mission to stay stupid. After 180 school days of systematic mental torture, I was ready to see the end of him.

I was determined to ignore Kevin and make some progress on a conjecture people had been trying to prove since 1742. What can I say? I like a challenge.

Kevin let off one more shot, but when I didn't react, he refocused his attentions on a trio of girls at the back of the classroom. He leaned his head back, calculating the arc the little paper missiles would have to take to clear the four rows of desks between him and his target and the force he'd have to put behind them.

Then he blew.

For someone who got straight Ds in math, he seemed to understand the practical applications of a parabola just fine. Squeals and screams erupted from the back of the room as the spitballs rained down. He must have loaded the straw with about a dozen of the things.

"Mr. Jordan." Mrs. Wright stood up from her desk. Her

curly hair was frazzled beyond recognition in the damp heat and it made her look more than a bit deranged.

Kevin smiled like an angel. You could practically see the halo of innocence over his blond curls. But Mrs. Wright was immune.

"You know the drill." She pointed to the door.

Mrs. Wright watched him saunter out of the classroom, on his way to the wooden bench outside the principal's office. When he graduated (*if* he graduated) they'd have to put up a brass plate naming that bench in his honor. The door closed behind him, and Mrs. Wright turned her gaze on me. She shook her head in that weary way adults do, like somehow Kevin Jordan shooting spitballs was all my fault. I just gritted my teeth and got back to the conjecture.

I didn't get far.

Sitting on top of my notebook was a perfectly folded triangle of blue-lined notebook paper. I looked around quickly. I'm not the kind of girl people pass notes to.

Two desks back and one desk over, Sammy Delgado Jr. gave me a small wave. Sammy was a small kid with dark hair and matching smudges beneath his eyes. Before Christmas, I don't think Sammy and I had ever really spoken. I'm not exactly a people person. But everyone at school knows, when it comes to figuring things out, I'm your girl.

3

So when Sammy had a problem he couldn't solve, he came to me for help.

Mysteries are a lot like math, word problems especially. Some are simple, some are complicated, but it's the same process. There's something you want to know, and a lot of information swimming around. The hard part is coming up with the right equation, figuring out which bits of information are important and which bits are just there to confuse you. Then it's just a matter of solving for x.

In Sammy's case, the equation had gone something like this:

$$\text{(strange scratching sounds in the night)} +$$
$$\text{(super-spooky house)} = x$$

When Sammy had done the math, he'd come up with ghosts. But it hadn't taken me long to figure out that those ghosts were actually a family of squirrels living in one of the house's many secret passageways. I'd closed the case and earned one very persistent fan.

I unfolded the note.

TOP SECRET: FOR YOUR EYES ONLY
Hi Alice,
Remember I told you I was helping Dr.
Learner with his research? Well, we made
a huge breakthrough. Dad's announcing it

today. You have to come. I can't say what
it is, because it's top secret, but you
won't believe your eyes! It'll be great!

Sammy

P.S. You can ride home with me after
school. My dad's sending a car.

P.P.S. Destroy this note after you read it.

Sammy had been asking me to come over for months, and
I'd been saying no for just as long. Now it was the last day of
school before summer vacation, and he was getting his dad
involved. Sammy just didn't know when to give up.

Sammy's dad runs a science laboratory called Delgado
Industries. It's not as if I wasn't interested. I'd have loved to
see inside a real lab. But Delgado Industries was notoriously
secretive, so I didn't believe for one second that Sammy was
allowed anywhere near the actual research. Sammy had hinted
that his "Top Secret" research was all about turning invisible.
I was pretty sure Sammy's project was something his dad had
dreamed up to keep him busy after school. People have been
trying to develop invisibility technology for years. If Sammy
Delgado Jr. was the one to finally figure it out, I'd eat my hat.

I crumpled the note and stuffed it inside my desk. It looked
like I'd be sneaking out the back. If Sammy really had invented some way to turn invisible, it would be a lot easier to ignore

him. Then again, if he could turn invisible, how would I know he wasn't standing next to me all the time? I shivered slightly at the thought, then shook my head clear. Invisibility was something out of science fiction, not fact.

The final bell rang and I stood with the rest of the class, sliding my notebook back into my backpack and slinging the whole mess over my shoulder. I made tracks for the door before Sammy could ask if I'd gotten his message. But I wasn't quite fast enough.

"Hey, Alice, wait up." Sammy's high voice carried over the crowd, even though I couldn't see him anymore. I walked faster, weaving through the crush of bodies that lined the halls. Why people are unable to leave in an orderly manner is beyond me, but for once the chaos worked in my favor. I'm not tall, but I had no problem elbowing my way through the crowd. Sammy is a good four inches shorter than me, and not nearly as pushy. His calls got quieter and quieter as he was buffeted back and forth like he was stuck in a pinball machine.

I ducked around the corner into the school's second entrance hall, the one at the far end of the parking lot. It was a large square room with a worn red carpet. The guidance counselor's office was on the left and the principal's office (and Kevin Jordan's bench, featuring Kevin Jordan) was on the right. Outside, the rain was coming down in sheets. I could have waited for the rain to let up, but the thought of running into Sammy was even less appealing than getting soaked to the bone on the ride home. I dug out the key to my bike lock and braced myself to make a run for it.

"Hey, Numbers, have fun in the rain."

"Thanks, Kevin. Have fun getting told off by the principal."

"Will do." He grinned.

I rolled my eyes and ran into the rain, counting my steps as I went. In three steps I was damp, at ten my shoes were starting to squelch, and by the time I got to my bike (thirty-eight steps) I felt like I'd been thrown in a pool. It took me three tries to get my bike lock open. The slick metal kept sliding through my fingers.

I was winding up the chain when I noticed them. They emerged from the rain like actors stepping onstage from behind a curtain. Two men the size of gorillas wearing matching black suits. Their ties were black as well, too skinny for their broad frames. The man on the left carried an oversized black umbrella, but they looked more than a little uncomfortable to be sharing it. What I noticed most about them, though, was that they were looking straight at me.

I put my head down and finished putting away my bike lock, doing my best to ignore the two pairs of shoes that appeared in front of me.

"Alice Jones?" one of them grunted. I couldn't tell which one.

"Who wants to know?" I asked. A drop of water ran down the tip of my nose and hung there.

"Mr. Delgado would like to see you."

"Mr. Delgado? Sammy's dad? Tell him to make an appointment." I didn't like the man's tone.

Apparently, he didn't like mine either.

Before I knew what was happening, I felt a sharp jerk on the back of my shirt, and my feet lifted ever so slightly off the ground. I dropped my bike and tried to twist free, but it was no good.

"Hey!" I shouted as they frog-marched me toward the open door of a black town car.

I swung my arms, trying to get some momentum, but the man holding me was the size of a small country and no amount of force on my part was going to move him. At least not conventional force. Instead of trying to break free, I grabbed on, wrapping my legs around his and locking my feet together on the other side. Without his feet to balance and with me holding on to him, he went down like a giant redwood. Unfortunately, I went down too, and I went down hard. I hit the concrete back first. The air rushed out of me and no amount of gasping seemed to get any back in.

I was vaguely aware of the rain hitting my face and a lot of swearing in my ear. Then I was lifted like a sack of potatoes and the world turned upside down. I could see feet running toward me, splashing through the puddles that stretched across the parking lot reflecting the stormy sky. With his plastic raincoat billowing out behind him, he looked like an avenging angel swooping in to save me, which was hilarious. If I could have breathed, I would have died laughing.

(2

I OPENED MY eyes to find Sammy staring down at me. We were in the backseat of the car and we were moving.

"You're awake." His dopey smile and overeager eyes made my head ache.

"Sammy, they got you too?"

I sat up slowly, my back protesting, but at least I could breathe now.

"I always get a ride home," Sammy said. And then it hit me. I'd been ignoring Sammy for so long, he'd asked his dad to make me come over. What was wrong with this kid?

"I'm so excited. I can't wait for my dad to meet you. I told him all about how you solved the mystery of the ghost in the wall. He was really impressed."

"I'll bet he was."

Sammy grinned at me and sat on his hands, fidgeting back

and forth like a four-year-old trying to keep a secret. "Oh, wow. I can't wait to see the look on your face when Dad makes the announcement about Dr. Learner's new invention. You are gonna be so amazed. I helped Dr. Learner make the breakthrough, you know." He stopped talking long enough to take a short breath, then kept right on going. "But don't tell anyone. I'm not supposed to go in the lab. You destroyed the note, right? Dad says there are spies everywhere."

"Sounds like some invention," I said as I leaned to the side to look out the front window.

We were driving out of town on Route 30 toward the Main Line. It was the beginning of rush hour and traffic was barely crawling. I jiggled the door handle. It didn't open. The two men in suits had turned on the child locks. I named the driver Bruno and the other man Brutus. I had a feeling they wouldn't be introducing themselves.

"For your safety," Bruno said without turning around. I resisted the urge to kick the back of his seat. I had to count to 211 (the forty-seventh prime number).

What kind of dad sends two goons to pick up his son from school and kidnap one of his classmates? And why didn't Sammy think it was weird? I wondered if he got all his friends this way.

"Great," I said under my breath. "Just great."

"I know, isn't it!"

I pulled my phone out of my backpack and sent my dad a text to let him know where I was. I didn't want him to freak out and call the police when I didn't come home. He writes the Crime Report for the *Philadelphia Daily News*. He likes to have the cops owing him favors, not the other way around. Then I put my head against the window and watched the city melt into the suburbs.

We pulled up a mile-long driveway and stopped right in front of the Delgado Mansion. It was a large square building with the kind of windows that watched you. Long, grasping arms of ivy crawled up the walls. I'd only been there once before, when I'd solved Sammy's squirrel mystery. It had been a beautiful sunny day, but even then the house had looked creepy. This time it was even worse. Lightning flashed, thunder crashed. All that was missing were some screeching bats. Sammy and I waited while the muscle up front opened the doors for us. Bruno held the umbrella out for Sammy and took his bag. Brutus opened my door and grunted.

"Still sore?" I asked. The man didn't say anything, but the way he glared at me was more than eloquent. I climbed out of the car and into the downpour without help.

As I ran past Sammy across the gravel driveway, a large white van pulled in and parked next to a small line of cars by the entrance of the house. The words CHANNEL 4 ACTION NEWS were printed in bold blue letters across the side.

I made it up the steps to the front door just in time for it to swing open, almost knocking me back into the rain. A man in his mid-twenties wearing a dark-gray suit that was exactly the right size stared down at me like he'd just found something unpleasant on the bottom of his shoe. He had an umbrella in one hand and two more hooked over his arm.

He sniffed once, then lifted his umbrella and walked quickly into the rain toward the van. Sammy shied slightly as the man brushed past him.

"What's going on here?" I asked Sammy as he came up the steps.

Sammy looked at the camera van and back at me. He grinned so hard it looked like it hurt.

"I told you! Dad's announcing Dr. Learner's new invention." He puffed out his chest. "Come on, what are you waiting for? This is going to be so great."

Sammy shot through the door without a second glance at the camera crew. Maybe it wasn't just his imagination after all. I took one last look over my shoulder at the driveway, but my bike was back at school and I doubted Bruno or Brutus would give me a ride home. I sighed and followed Sammy inside.

The entrance hall was palatial and arctic. From the walls to the paintings on them, the entire room was decorated in varying shades of white. It was like standing inside a very large and well-decorated igloo. I stood shivering in my shoes and dripping onto the white marble floor. Mr. Delgado was not a man who believed in skimping on the AC.

Sammy checked his watch. "OK, there's still time. Let's go to my room. We can have snacks before it starts." He grabbed my arm and started to drag me toward the large curved staircase that dominated the room, but stopped short. There was a good puddle of water pooling around my shoes. From the look on Sammy's face, I guessed water wasn't welcome in the Delgado household.

"Oh, right. Just wait here. I'll bring a towel. Be right back." Sammy was halfway up the stairs, but he kept talking. "I've got bathrobes for us too. They match. It'll be great!" He yelled the last line as he reached the top step and then disappeared down the hallway.

I shivered a little harder, and it had nothing to do with the cold. Hanging out with Sammy was bad enough, but matching bathrobes? Scientific breakthrough or not, that was taking things too far. I'd rather walk home through a tsunami.

"If you need us, we'll be right outside," Brutus grunted. "Have fun." Then he and Bruno walked back out the front door. I was pretty sure that was Brutus's way of saying "Don't try to make a run for it." At least, that's what his smirk made me think. If I wanted to get out of the Delgado Mansion, I'd have to find another way.

Besides the stairs going up and the front door going out, there were five other exits out of the entrance hall. My sneakers squelched against the marble tiles as I made my way quickly across the floor. The first door I opened was a closet. The next one was a bathroom. I grabbed one of the monogrammed hand towels and dried myself off a little. It didn't help the squelching, but at least it stopped the water from running into my eyes.

I opened the third door expecting to find another dead end. Instead, I found myself staring into a room full of people. The room stared back. I could tell by the way the conversation ground to a halt that they weren't expecting to see a dripping-wet twelve-year-old girl. I smiled as best as I could and moved to the side of the room. The key to blending in is pretending you belong. Nine times out of ten, if you act like you're supposed to be somewhere, people believe you. With any luck, I could hide out in the crowd until Bruno and Brutus gave up their guard duty and then make a break for it.

The room looked like the study on a space station. The floors and walls and furniture were all silver or white, and smooth as if they'd been designed for speed by a team of engineers. The bookshelves that lined the walls to my left were almost transparent, giving the illusion that the books were floating in midair. To my right, three flat-screen TVs embedded into the wall displayed the Delgado Industries logo. A row of trophies sat in a proud line on the cupboard beneath them. Apparently, Delgado Industries had been runner-up for the American Excellence in Scientific Research Award for the past five years. The only things in the room that looked like they came from this century were the folding chairs. There were eighteen of them, three rows of six, all facing the grand white desk at the front of the room.

The reporters forgot about me before the door was even shut and went back to speaking in excited whispers, each trying to get more information from their neighbor than they were giving away themselves. I could feel the excitement building, charging the air like a thunderstorm. Even I was intrigued. It would have to be a pretty big announcement to get reporters this worked up. As long as Sammy and his bathrobe didn't show up, this might be interesting.

I made my way across the room to a refreshment table molded out of pearlescent white plastic. It took me a moment to find the coffee in a large metal urn shaped like a rocket. I poured myself a cup and started looking through the books on the shelves. They were all autobiographies and science books. I'd just pulled out *Feynman Lectures on Computation* when a voice made me jump.

"What's a nice girl like you doing in a place like this?"

I spun around, sloshing hot coffee all over my hand. I managed to keep the book safe and put it back quickly.

16

"Dad? What are you doing here?"

Dad grabbed a bunch of napkins and began to mop up the coffee dripping down my arm. It was hard to tell where the coffee ended and the rainwater began, but he did his best.

"I'm covering for Greico from Science and Technology. She's been going on about this announcement for months. It's supposed to be a pretty big deal. Look, even Channel Four came." Dad refilled my cup and we found two seats next to each other. "The question is, what are *you* doing here?"

I made myself as comfortable as you can when your clothes are soaked through. Dad sat down. Then he stood up to get his notebook out of his back pocket and sat down again.

"Mr. Delgado's personal henchmen picked me up from school."

"I know. I got your text." He flipped through the notebook until he found a blank page, got a pencil out, licked it, and began tapping the point against the paper. "But why?" Dad adjusted his glasses and raised his eyebrows at me. "Don't tell me Sammy kidnapped you for a playdate."

I rolled my eyes. "No, he wanted me to come to this press conference. He said he helped make the breakthrough. Just let me hang out here until you can give me a ride home."

Dad made a face like he was impressed.

"I'm pretty sure he was exaggerating. He probably held a notepad or something."

"Maybe you should give the kid a break. You know what your mom says about making new friends."

"Dad. It's Sammy."

"Maybe if you gave him a chance, he wouldn't be so bad."

"No, Dad, it's Sammy. He's over there." Sammy stood in the doorway wearing a maroon paisley dressing gown with satin lapels. He looked like he'd walked straight out of a Sherlock Holmes novel. All that was missing was the pipe. He had more maroon paisley draped over his arm. Paisley meant for me. I hunkered down in my chair and tried to make myself invisible.

"So that's Sammy?" Dad whistled softly. "You said he helped with some of Dr. Learner's experiments?"

"Dad, please don't. Sammy asked me to keep it a secret."

"Don't worry, I'll be discreet," Dad said as he stood up and waved at Sammy.

At first Sammy just looked confused, but then Dad pointed at me and motioned Sammy over, scooting me down a seat so we could all sit together. Dad would talk to anyone for a story. Even if Sammy was just a fly on the wall while Dr. Learner was conducting his experiments, he was still a source. Normally, I wouldn't mind, but this time he was getting me involved.

"Hi, Alice. Here's your bathrobe. I was worried I wouldn't find you before the press conference started." I don't think

Sammy even realized I'd been trying to get away. He glanced around the room and licked his lips, then leaned into my personal space and whispered, "You are not going to believe your eyes. Dr. Learner said his invention could change the world!"

I was saved from any more conversation, and from Dad starting to ask questions, by Mr. Delgado himself. He made his entrance through the door behind the desk and stood in the doorway, his body almost filling the frame, until he had our attention. He was one of those men who owned a room. Everything about him was designed to impress, from the mirror-shine on his expensive shoes to the perfectly groomed hair parted on one side and brushed across the top of his head, not one strand out of place. Even though he hadn't said a word, we were all watching him.

Mr. Delgado stepped into the room and smoothed his hand over his hair. For just a moment, I wondered if he was nervous. I looked at Sammy, but he didn't seem worried.

Mr. Delgado centered himself behind his desk and looked out at the crowd, gathering us up with his eyes. And when he was certain he had our full attention, he started to speak.

"Ladies and gentlemen, I'm afraid the unveiling of the latest scientific breakthrough, which Delgado Industries made in December, cannot go ahead as scheduled."

A dull murmur filled the room as Mr. Delgado paused for

dramatic effect. Out of the corner of my eye, I saw Sammy lick his lips. He suddenly looked nervous. "Instead, I have a much more serious announcement to make. Our top scientist, and lead researcher on this project, Dr. Adrian Learner, has disappeared."

3

THE ROOM ERUPTED into a storm of shouted questions, each journalist trying to be heard above the crowd. Pencils scratched and keyboards clicked.

"What do you mean, Dr. Learner's disappeared?"

"Are you working with the police?"

"Do you suspect foul play?"

"Was there an accident in the lab? Is this some sort of cover-up?"

Dad scribbled shorthand in his notebook so fast his pencil was a blur. He'd already filled three pages when he stood up and asked his first question.

"Is it true that Dr. Learner was experimenting with invisibility?" he asked, projecting his voice above the crowd.

As soon as my dad said the word *invisibility*, the volume in the room tripled. My stomach flipped. I was sure I hadn't said anything about what kind of research Dr. Learner and Sammy were working on. Why would I? I hadn't believed a word of it. But that didn't stop me from feeling guilty. I turned toward Sammy, but he wasn't paying any attention. He was just staring off into the distance, worry lines growing across his face.

Mr. Delgado's eyes darted to the group of chairs at the back of the audience. I turned in my seat to get a better look. In the last row, a group of men and women in plain gray suits sat like statues. They definitely weren't reporters. I looked closer. The two sitting closest to me—a woman with red hair pulled back in a neat braid and a middle-aged man with a crew cut—had small metal pins fastened to their lapels. But I was too far away to see what they were.

For a moment, it looked like Mr. Delgado was going to deny everything, but he didn't.

"Yes," he said slowly. Then, choosing each word as carefully as you choose a surgeon, he continued, "I can confirm that Dr. Learner's research focused on invisibility."

The sudden silence in the room made my ears ring.

"Did Dr. Learner disappear because he completed his research? Or did his research cause him to disappear?" Dad asked, his pencil poised to write down whatever Mr. Delgado said. I could feel the whole room leaning forward, waiting for the answer.

Mr. Delgado smoothed his hand over his hair again. A ghost of a smile lifted the corners of his mouth and then vanished just as quickly. I frowned. I couldn't help feeling like Mr. Delgado was making this a lot more dramatic than it needed to be.

"I'm afraid at the moment it's impossible for me to answer that question. You see, when Dr. Learner disappeared, all of his research disappeared with him."

Sammy gasped and grabbed hold of my hand. His fingers were damp with sweat. I slid my palm free and wiped it on my leg. I couldn't tell if he was just caught up in his dad's performance, or if he was really worried. Either way, I wasn't going to hold his hand.

"And this was no ordinary disappearance." Mr. Delgado pressed a button on the top of his desk and the large painting behind him slowly rose into the ceiling, revealing the largest TV screen I'd ever seen. Then he stepped to one side and nodded to his assistant to dim the lights.

A picture of a door and a small slice of hallway flickered onto the screen. The muted black-and-white picture was clearly from a security camera. The date and time were displayed in the bottom right corner: 4:00 p.m. yesterday afternoon. Nothing happened for a moment, then a man in a dull-gray lab coat walked down the hall. He hunched over, clutching a pile of papers tightly to his chest and looking over his shoulder as if someone was close behind him. It was hard to see the details of his face, but the way his hands shook as he tried to unlock the door made me pretty sure he didn't want to see whoever it was.

I could feel Sammy holding his breath, waiting to see who came next. But no one did.

Mr. Delgado stepped forward and pressed another button on his desk, fast-forwarding the video. Two lines of static striped across the screen, but the image didn't change at all.

"Yesterday at four p.m., Dr. Adrian Learner went into his office. He never came back out. We have security camera footage of Dr. Learner entering his office, but no footage of him leaving. His office only has one door, and there are no windows."

The static lines stopped. I checked the timestamp at the bottom of the screen: 7:00 a.m.

"When his lab assistant went to find him this morning, Dr. Learner was gone."

Mr. Delgado let the tape play for a few more minutes, and we all watched as a large man stepped into the frame and knocked on Dr. Learner's door. He knocked again, and then, after a few minutes, walked back up the hallway. Mr. Delgado motioned for the lights, stepped behind his desk, and pressed a button. The painting slid back down from the ceiling, covering the frozen image of Dr. Learner's office door.

As soon as the lights came up, the questions started again,

even louder than before. Mr. Delgado did his best to answer the questions he could hear above the rest, but it was like trying to outrun a train. It didn't take long before Mr. Delgado started to run out of steam.

"Are you sure no one tampered with the tape?"

Mr. Delgado was sure.

"Is this some sort of publicity stunt?"

Sadly, no, this was very real and very serious.

"Do you think Dr. Learner has taken his research to one of your competitors?"

Mr. Delgado's face flushed red. "Absolutely not! Dr. Learner is not only a valued member of Delgado Industries, he is also a close personal friend. I went to school with Adrian, and I know he would never leave of his own free will. If he or his research is found with another laboratory, I am positive they will have been taken by force." Mr. Delgado's voice broke slightly. He took a moment to compose himself before continuing. "That is why I am asking for your help. Delgado Industries is offering a ten-thousand-dollar reward for any information that leads to Dr. Learner's safe return."

As if responding to some preplanned cue, Mr. Delgado's assistant stepped forward and took the floor.

"That will be all for today," he said. His voice was cool and emotionless. "Mr. Delgado has many urgent matters to attend to and will not be answering any further questions. There are press kits with background information and further details at the back of the room. Thank you for your time."

All the reporters in the room started talking at once, protesting loudly that they still had questions. My dad perched on the edge of his seat, waving his hand in the air. I could almost see him writing the headline MYSTERIOUS DISAPPEARANCE OF TOP SCIENTIST. It was a sensational story, like something from a movie.

I was curious too, and not just about the scientist. Ever since Mr. Delgado announced Dr. Learner and his research had gone missing, Sammy had been fidgeting in his chair like it was made of ants. He'd been so excited for me to come to this press conference and see the "invisibility breakthrough" he'd helped discover. I could understand him being disappointed or worried. But he wasn't acting like that. He was acting guilty, and I couldn't figure out why.

"Mr. Delgado, Mr. Delgado," the reporters clamored, but Mr. Delgado didn't say another word. He let his assistant lead him through the private door behind the desk and disappeared.

"Well, that was interesting," I said, standing up. All around me the other reporters were shuffling to the back of the room, collecting their press kits and making for the door, ears pressed to their phones as they called in the story. It was a race now to see which paper could get the story posted first. The four suited statues were nowhere to be seen. I wondered who they were and what they were doing at the press conference, but I didn't say anything. I didn't want to stick around any longer than I had to. "Come on, Dad. We should head home."

"What a story!" Dad wasn't listening to me. "A scientist working on invisibility technology goes missing. This has 'front page' written all over it." He looked up at the ceiling, waiting for inspiration to strike. "TOP INVISIBILITY SCIENTIST DISAPPEARS . . . OR DOES HE?" He frowned. "Oh, oh, I've got it! NOW YOU SEE HIM, NOW YOU DON'T: LEADING INVISIBILITY EXPERT DISAPPEARS." He quickly scribbled the two headlines in his Moleskine notebook, dotting the last line with enough force to make a sound. "I'm going to go see if I can get Mr. Delgado to answer a few more questions, off the record."

I sighed. Dad had the story bug. It looked like I'd be cooking dinner tonight. When Dad's on the scent of a good story, he doesn't even know I exist. He doesn't know anyone exists. It's just him and the words, and a bottle of water he chugs from like he's running a marathon. When my mom left, he was in the middle of an article about police corruption. He didn't even notice she'd gone until two days later when he ran out of clean socks.

While Dad worked his way to the front of the room, I moved to the back and poured myself another cup of coffee. Most of my first one had ended up on me, not in me, and on a day like this, one coffee just wasn't enough. Sammy tagged along behind me, but he didn't say a word. It was the longest I'd ever seen him be quiet, which was typical. People always clam up when you want answers.

"So, Sammy, I know you wanted it to be a surprise, but what exactly was this breakthrough you and Dr. Learner made?" I asked.

It took Sammy a moment to realize I'd asked him a question. He started slightly. "I'm not supposed to say, not until Dad makes an official announcement." He scrunched up his face like keeping the secret physically hurt. "But it's really amazing. Dr. Learner is super-smart."

I watched Dad trying to get past Mr. Delgado's assistant. My dad was usually pretty good at getting what he wanted, but the assistant was better. Dad's charm didn't even make a dent. I wondered what Mr. Delgado's lab worked on besides invisibility. The real science, not the sensational stuff designed to get headlines. Maybe they developed androids. If someone told me Dad was talking to the prototype, I'd almost believe them.

"Do you know Dr. Learner well?" I asked.

"Oh, yeah, we hang out all the time. And he helps me with my science fair projects. He's great!" Sammy's voice trailed off. "I hope he's OK."

Most people would just say, "I'm sure he's fine," but I had no idea what had happened to Dr. Learner, and I don't like lying to people. So I said nothing and took a sip of coffee. Sammy stared up at me. I didn't like the hopeful sheen in his eye.

"Maybe you could find him, Alice? You're great at solving mysteries."

I nearly choked. Sammy's eyes went from hopeful glow to full-on blaze. I looked around, hoping my dad was well out of earshot, but it was too late. He was already right behind me, listening to the words fall out of Sammy's mouth. "I can help you. We'll be a team. It'll be great!"

"Sammy, I don't think . . ." I started, but Dad cut me off.

"I don't know, Alice, maybe you should give it a try. You *are* very good at figuring things out." He grinned at me. There was no escape. "But," Dad said to Sammy, "we should really talk with your father first."

"Good idea." Sammy nodded vigorously. "Let's go."

I was going to put my foot down. I did not want to spend my summer playing detective with Sammy Delgado.

"Dad . . ." I started.

"Oh, come on, Alice," he said. "It won't hurt to talk to the guy." Dad wiggled his eyebrows at me, and I knew I'd lost.

I was being managed and I didn't like it. But they were right. There was no real reason to say no, just a gut feeling that I'd regret it.

"Fine," I said. "I'll talk to Mr. Delgado. It's not like he's going to want me to help anyway."

(4

"FOLLOW ME," SAMMY said, and led us out of the study and back into the entrance hall.

"Uh, Sammy, didn't your father go the other way?" Dad asked.

"Oh, there's another door out of that room. Dad uses it to avoid the reporters. This way."

"Why doesn't your dad just hold press conferences at his lab?" I asked as we followed him through a small doorway.

The hall on the other side was dim compared to the white marble entrance hall, but it was still clearly designed to impress. Large gold-framed paintings lined the walls, and the carpet was so thick it muffled our footsteps into near-silence.

Sammy looked at me like I'd asked him the square root of negative one.

"Dad takes security very seriously. The lab is working on all sorts of top-secret projects. There's no way Dad would let in a bunch of reporters. One of them might be a spy or something." His mouth froze in the shape of an O, and he looked quickly at my dad. "Not that I think you're a spy, Mr. Jones. I mean . . . what I meant was . . ."

Dad cut him off before he could start hyperventilating. "Don't worry about it, Sammy. I know what you meant. But I bet you know how to get around all the security systems at the lab, don't you? After all, you were Dr. Learner's assistant."

I elbowed Dad in the ribs. So much for being discreet. But Sammy didn't seem to notice; he just hurried down the hallway a bit more quickly.

We passed three doors before Sammy stopped and opened a fourth, leading us into a large open living room.

Four identical couches were arranged in the middle of the room, back-to-back and perpendicular to a large marble fireplace. Over the fireplace was a giant painting of Mr. Delgado himself, draped in black academic robes with a flash of gold silk lining. The faint smell of oil paint hung in the air. On either side of the fireplace, the walls were filled with smaller gold-framed photographs. I thought they'd be family portraits, but they weren't. They were all pictures of Mr. Delgado shaking hands with the cream of Philadelphia society.

Mr. Delgado stood in one of the large windows. For a moment, I thought he was looking at something outside. Then

I realized he was checking his reflection in the glass. He frowned, brushed his eyebrows back into place, and turned from side to side, sucking in his stomach.

"Dad," Sammy said. Mr. Delgado jumped guiltily, turning to see who was there. Dad had already stepped away from me and Sammy and was moving along the wall, checking out each picture one at a time. I don't think he wanted Mr. Delgado to know he was there, not until he got a feel for him.

"Sammy." Mr. Delgado swallowed hard. The circumference of his collar was smaller than the circumference of his neck, and the extra roll of skin quivered. "I told you not to interrupt me while I'm working."

"But Dad, it's important."

"Sammy, I'm very busy right now. I don't have time for your nonsense." Mr. Delgado tugged at his cuffs and straightened his cuff links. His shirt was so perfectly white, I wondered if he'd bought it just for the press conference. He glanced at me. "Why don't you and your little friend go play in your room?"

I gritted my teeth. I'd figured out what kind of dad kidnaps friends for his son—a bad one.

"But Dad," Sammy said, pointing at me like I was something on a shelf, "this is Alice. She's really good at solving mysteries. She can help find Dr. Learner."

Mr. Delgado snorted. "I hardly think this is a place for a

girl to get involved, Sammy. Now do me a favor and stop pestering me."

Sammy glanced at me and then turned away, but not before I'd seen his red face and wet eyes. Mr. Delgado saw them too. He scowled at Sammy and stepped across the space between them. His shoes were so highly polished they flashed as they caught the light. I hoped he'd put anti-slip pads on the soles, or he was asking for a fall.

"Are you crying?" He leaned over Sammy until their faces were just inches apart. I couldn't tell if he wanted me to hear what he said or not. But if he didn't, he needed to talk a lot softer.

Sammy shook his head. I turned my back and stared at the windows. It was too painful to watch.

"What have I told you about crying? It makes you look weak. Do you think I got to where I am today by looking weak?"

Sammy didn't answer, but I imagined him shaking his head again, even more miserably.

"Do you think you get to live in this nice house and have nice things because I cried when things were tough?"

"No, sir." Sammy sniffed.

"No. I didn't. Now go to your room until you can control yourself."

Sammy wiped his nose with the back of his arm. He took one last look at me and then fled. He ran so hard I could actually hear his footsteps on that thick carpet in the hall.

Mr. Delgado looked at me. "I'm sorry you had to see that. I'd appreciate it if you didn't tell the other children at school about this." I wasn't sure if he wanted me to keep quiet about him being a jerk or about Sammy crying. Probably about Sammy crying. People like Mr. Delgado never even realize they're being jerks. People like Mr. Delgado think they're great no matter what evidence you have that proves otherwise. He reached into his back pocket and pulled out his wallet, like he was going to pay me to keep my mouth shut.

"That's OK," I said, shaking my head as he held out a twenty. I didn't like Mr. Delgado, and I didn't want his money. I just wanted to get out of there.

Mr. Delgado looked at me, then at the twenty, confused. I guess most people took the money. After a moment he put it back in his wallet. If I'd had my way, that would have been the end of it. Mr. Delgado didn't want any help, fine by me. Let him find his precious scientist on his own and let me out of there. The case might have been interesting, and I felt a twinge of guilt about Sammy, but it wasn't up to me to fix his family problems.

My dad had other ideas. He'd finished looking at all of the pictures of Mr. Delgado and his famous friends, and now made his way to the middle of the room.

"Are you sure you don't want her help, Mr. Delgado?" he asked. "Alice is very clever. She's helped me on lots of cases."

Mr. Delgado turned around quickly to see who else was in

34

the room. He didn't look happy. I wondered if he'd try to pay my dad to keep quiet too. And if he'd offer him more than twenty bucks.

"And you would be . . . ?" he asked.

"Arthur Jones, *Philadelphia Daily News*. I'm Alice's father." Dad pointed at one of the photos. "Is this you and the mayor?"

Mr. Delgado lost his frown in a hurry as soon as he heard the word *news*. He shook my dad's hand and smiled like he was accepting an award. I guess he didn't want Dad writing any stories about the lousy way he spoke to his kid. "Yes, that's the mayor. I hosted a little dinner for some local businesses and politicians this fall. It was quite a success, if I do say so myself. Although we didn't get the press coverage we deserved." He smiled ruefully. "But I guess that's what happens when you have to keep the most exciting details of your work a secret."

"It sounds like you make some very challenging decisions for the good of your company. Great men are seldom recognized in their time," Dad said. "I hope you'll forgive me for barging in on you like this. Sammy wanted to introduce you to Alice, and I'm afraid I couldn't resist tagging along. I so wanted to meet you."

Mr. Delgado practically glowed. "No need to apologize. I completely understand. I didn't get named Philadelphia Businessman of the Year playing by the rules. We make our own luck in this life, isn't that right?"

"How very true," Dad agreed.

Mr. Delgado turned slowly to look at me again, and this time he smiled. I gritted my teeth harder. It was like being stared at by a snake.

"Of course! How foolish of me. You aren't just any Alice. You're Alice *Jones*," he said, like somehow that made all the difference in the world. "Sammy certainly has told me a lot about you."

"I'll bet," I said drily, wishing I'd never taken Sammy's squirrel case.

"Well, well, well, isn't this interesting." He sat back down on one of the couches and patted the seat for me to sit beside him. I didn't budge. I didn't like where this was going one bit. I could almost read the headlines Mr. Delgado was making up in his head.

"Sammy and your father seem to think you just might be able to help me find my friend." He leaned forward and rested his elbows on his knees like he was talking to a three-year-old. "So what do you say? Will you help me? Will you take the case?"

"You do realize I'm twelve?"

Mr. Delgado laughed like a barking seal. "Ah, good, very good," he said, wiping the damp corners of his eyes. "Yes, I'm well aware of your age. Don't worry, there are other people searching for Dr. Learner and his research as well. I've hired the best private investigator in Pennsylvania to search for

Dr. Learner." He paused, his face darkening. "And I'm sure that other laboratories who want to get their hands on the invisibility su—" He caught himself just in time. "Excuse me, Dr. Learner's research. They will be looking for him too. Alice, you might be the key to bringing my friend home safely. You have a certain . . . visibility that might be useful."

"So you don't actually want me to find Dr. Learner, you just want me to pretend to be looking for him to keep the press interested." The bottoms of my feet were starting to itch from standing too long in wet socks. I shifted from one foot to the other and tried not to look too annoyed.

"She is bright, isn't she?" Mr. Delgado spoke to my dad over my shoulder like I wasn't even in the room. Then he turned back to me. "Of course I wouldn't expect a young girl like you to actually be able to *find* Dr. Learner, but by helping to look for him you would keep the story in the papers. And if a member of the public reads the story and sends us a tip, well, that would almost be like you solving the mystery all by yourself."

He smiled at me. A big, wide, patronizing smile.

"So what do you say, will you help me? In fact, I'll even give you a head start." He opened a small, thin drawer in the table beside the couch and pulled out a manila folder. He waved it at me like it was some sort of treat. "These are the full details of the case. I was saving this for the private investigator I've hired, but I can make him another copy. I'm sure you'll be discreet.

And, of course, I'll add your name to the authorized visitor list at Delgado Industries so you can check out the scene of the crime."

I looked Mr. Delgado up and down, from his fancy haircut to his handmade shoes. He was the kind of man who was used to getting his own way. Part of me wanted to turn him down flat, just to see the look on his face. But I didn't. I had a better idea.

"Fine," I said. "I'll help you look for Dr. Learner."

Dad was across the room in two steps, and had the top-secret folder in his hands before I got the words out of my mouth. He grinned.

"Of course she'll do it. I will need to accompany her, though. She is only a minor, after all."

I could see dreams of insider access coming off my father in concentric rings. He shuffled me out of the room before Mr. Delgado had a chance to change his mind. Or maybe he was more worried about me. But I wasn't going to back out now.

I'd look for his missing scientist, and I'd find him too. No one uses me as a publicity stunt.

(5

AS WE WALKED back through the Delgados' entrance
hall, I tried to keep my dad between me and the stairs. I didn't
know how long it would take Sammy to recover from his dad's
scolding, but I didn't want to run into him if I didn't have to.
Dad was so busy thumbing through the manila folder, he didn't
notice until we were almost out of the door.

"Wait, are you using me as a human shield?" He stopped
just inside the door and stared down at me.

I grabbed the folder out of his hand and looked over his
shoulder up the stairs. No sign of Sammy yet. "I cover for you
when you're behind on a deadline."

Dad paused, thinking it over. "True," he said. "All right,
let's get out of here."

He didn't have to tell me twice. I was out the door before
he finished his sentence.

"Numbers!"

I stopped dead in my tracks, stumbling forward slightly when my dad walked into the back of me. It wasn't Sammy. It was worse. The voice came from behind one of the decorative columns that stood next to the front door pretending to hold up the front of the Delgado Mansion.

"Are you OK?" Kevin Jordan peered around the edge of the column, his cherub cheeks glowing in the rain.

"What are you doing here?" I asked.

"I saw those men grab you. I followed you. I rode your bike. We need to get out of here. Who's that?" The words tumbled out like marbles, clattering against each other. Kevin finally finished talking and stared suspiciously at my father.

"That's my dad," I said simply, and watched the confusion bloom on Kevin's face.

Maybe I should have been kinder and explained the whole situation. Kevin had obviously seen me get shoehorned into the back of Bruno and Brutus's car and tried to help out. Which was weird. Kevin Jordan hated me. I had the spitball marks to prove it. But I wasn't feeling kind. I stalked down the marble steps into the rain and across the large gravel drive to where the cars were parked.

It was easy to spot my dad's car, an ancient Plymouth station wagon, brick-colored with faded wood paneling on the doors.

It stood a little apart from all the other cars. Like they were embarrassed to get too close.

"Alice, who is this?" my dad asked, following me to the car.

"This is Kevin. He sits next to me at school." I opened the passenger door. The hinges screeched loud enough to be heard above the rain.

"Not Kevin the Spitball King?" Dad asked.

"That's the one."

"Well, well, well." My dad fixed Kevin with a devilish grin. "It might get you noticed, but it won't get you what you want. Come on, we'll give you a lift home. Put the bike in the back."

"Thanks, Mr. Jones," Kevin said quietly.

Kevin Jordan being polite to my dad. It was the strangest thing I'd heard all day.

We drove home in silence. Dad was thinking about his big story. His fingers drummed against the steering wheel like he was already typing copy. What he wasn't thinking about was the road. My dad drives like a maniac. I'm used to it, but for a first-timer like Kevin it must have been rough. I could actually hear his fingers crushing the cheap leather seat as he held on for dear life.

I almost felt sorry for him. But I had bigger things to worry about than Kevin Jordan. I'd just agreed to spend the summer playing detective, and I was pretty sure Sammy was going to want to tag along. I should have said no, but Mr. Delgado made me too angry to think straight. I sighed. It was too late to back out; I'd just have to do my best. At least Dad would be happy. He was getting first-class access to Delgado Industries.

From Sammy's, it was quicker to get to our house than to Kevin's. We live on Passfield Avenue, near South Street, so Dad dropped me off first. He stopped the Plymouth in the middle of the street and asked Kevin to get my bike out of the back.

I climbed out carefully, watching for traffic, and made my way around the car onto the sidewalk. It was littered with puddles.

Dad rolled down his window. "I'll be back soon. I'll pick up some dinner on my way home," he said.

Kevin handed me my bike and then took a step backward, away from Dad's car.

"I think I can walk home from here," he said when my dad waved for him to get back in.

"No, get in. I insist."

My dad was a hard man to say no to.

While Kevin got into the front seat and fastened his seat belt, Dad leaned out of the window and waved me closer.

"He seems nice." Dad winked at me. Then he pulled his head back into the car and drove away.

It had been a long day, the kind of day that called for a hot bath and a glass of cold milk. I trudged up the three concrete steps to our front door, dragging my bike beside me. I was still soaked to the bone, and shivering despite the muggy heat. The Delgados' air-conditioning system had done a real number on me. My fingers looked like raisins.

Our house was a small two-bedroom brick-fronted building. Wrought-iron bars protected the ground-floor windows from anyone who wanted to do more than have a peek inside. It wasn't much, but it was home. I shoved my key in the dead bolt, but it was already open, which was odd. Dad always locked the dead bolt. I used the second key on the Yale lock and slowly pushed it open.

The front door opened onto our combined living room and kitchen. Living room to the left. Kitchen to the right. A waist-high counter separated the two sections. The dead bolt being unlocked had put me on edge, or maybe I was just too tired to think properly. Whatever the reason, I noticed the refrigerator was open and I panicked.

I jumped around the corner of the counter to the kitchen side of the room and shouted, throwing my backpack at the shape crouching in front of the fridge. I immediately wished I hadn't. The shape was my twin sister, Della. Della screamed and jumped. The carton she'd been holding arced through the air in a low parabola: $y + x^2 = 0$. Then it hit the ground and exploded, showering me and Della and most of the downstairs in two-percent milk.

"What the heck, Alice?" Della said, flicking milk drops off her hands. Each flick was a miniature performance of her displeasure.

"Sorry," I said. "I'm so sorry. It's been one of those days."

When our parents split up a few years ago, Mom took Della and me with her to New York City. Mom's a costume designer. I fit in with her showbiz life like a pickle on an ice-cream sundae, so I learned how to do my own laundry and moved back to Philly to be with Dad. But Della loved the city. She'd always wanted to be a star on Broadway. She's gotten a few parts too. Orphan Number Three and First Street Urchin were among her finer performances.

Most summers, Della and Mom would go upstate to do summer stock theater productions, but this year Mom had gotten a job designing costumes for a new production of *The Magic Flute*. The problem was, the production was in Italy.

So this summer Della was staying with us. She'd been here for two days, and I was still getting used to it. It was hard to believe we shared a room until we were eight. I guess a lot can change in four years.

Della handed me a roll of paper towels, one eyebrow raised artfully. You could have seen it from the back of the house. It said, *You made this mess. You clean it up.*

Della is the older twin.

I started to sop up the milk while Della went upstairs to

change. We're fraternal twins, so we don't look that much alike. Della has honey-blonde hair that she styles so it bounces when she walks, like a little floating exclamation mark making all of her actions more dramatic. I'm blonde too, but it's the gingery variety. I wash my hair with whatever shampoo Dad has left in the shower and put it back in a braid while it's still wet. If I didn't know we were twins, I wouldn't believe we were even related.

As I scrubbed the floor, I could hear Della banging around my room. I'm not a neat freak, but I like to know where my things are. Della didn't have that problem. Her idea of unpacking was dumping her suitcase into the drawers I'd emptied out for her and asking me if I knew where she'd left her shoes. I think Mom still puts away Della's clean clothes.

"Alice," Della called down the stairs. Her voice was crystal clear, even through the closed door. My sister knew how to project. "Where are my socks?"

"Top drawer on the right," I yelled back.

It was going to be a long summer.

(6

I'D GOTTEN THE worst of the mess cleaned up by the time Dad came home. Della had come back downstairs and was sitting cross-legged on our brown corduroy couch doing deep-breathing exercises. Dad looked at us both and smiled.

"My two favorite girls together!" He paused, savoring the moment. I think Dad wished Della came to stay with us more often, but he wasn't the one who had to share a room with her. Dad put the takeout bag on the counter and began unpacking the food.

He'd gone to Pho Hoa, the Vietnamese restaurant up the street. The hot, tangy smell of lime juice and chilies began to fill the room. Dad's glasses fogged over from the steam.

"Smells great," I said. "What level did you get?"

Dad and I had been building up our spice tolerance since

the beginning of the year. I laid out three bowls at the end of the counter.

"Level four. Prepare yourself."

Della scrunched up her nose and looked worried.

"Uh, Dad," I said, checking the bag to see if there was another container. "Did you get a mild one for Della?"

Dad's face fell. "Oh, sweetie, I'm so sorry. I didn't think. Do you want me to go out and get you another one? It's just up the road."

"No. It's fine," Della said quickly. "We have spicy food in New York too . . ."

Maybe, I thought, but Dad and I had been working up to level four for months now.

I took a sip, the hot, sour soup burning all the way down the back of my throat. I could feel my sinuses clearing. It was just what I needed after the air-conditioning at the Delgado place.

"So, Della." Dad took a mouthful and then wiggled the empty spoon at my sister. "Any luck with the casting agent?"

Della smiled. "There's an open audition at the Walnut Street Theatre tomorrow. They're doing *Annie*."

I saw the flame in Della's eyes go from ember to bonfire. *Annie* was The Big One, the *Hamlet* of twelve-year-old theater girls. She took a triumphant spoonful of soup and immediately started to cough and splutter.

Level four was definitely not for beginners.

I got up to get her a glass of milk, but then I remembered there was no milk. Not anymore. Instead, I handed Della a slice of white bread. She stuffed it in her mouth and let it soak up the spice. Tears ran down her cheeks.

"I'm so sorry, sweetie. Why don't you let me go out and get you something else? Anything you like. Do you want me to go get some Italian ice?" Dad had his keys in his hand and was almost out of the door before Della managed to speak.

"Dad, I'm fine," Della wheezed. "I'll just have some toast. I shouldn't really eat anything spicy before an audition anyway." She poured her soup back into the Styrofoam cup and sealed the lid.

"Oh, of course not. I'm sorry. I wasn't thinking." Dad sat back down at the counter slowly. He always tried way too hard when Della came to visit and ended up getting mad at himself.

We sat in silence while Della put two slices of bread in the toaster. Awkward silence. I had some more soup and tried not to make any slurping sounds.

"Why don't you tell Della about the press conference?" I suggested. It was the best thing I could think of to make him feel better.

"Well," he said, "I guess it *was* pretty interesting."

Dad ran through the facts of the case, slowly at first, but picking up speed as he went.

"And then the scientist working on this top-secret invisibility project walked into his office and vanished without a trace. It was a locked room, with only one exit, and we know from the security cameras that Dr. Learner didn't come back out that way. But when his assistant went to look for him, he wasn't in his office."

"So someone messed with the security cameras," Della said, spreading peanut butter onto her toast.

"Ah, that's what I thought, but Mr. Delgado's assistant assured me that the security cameras are controlled by a professional security company in the city. And there's no way someone tampered with the recording." Dad slurped up a noodle and then wiped the drips off his chin.

Della sat back down at the counter. "Then there must be another way out of the office."

"Not according to the floor plan." Dad was enjoying himself now.

Della took a bite and chewed thoughtfully.

"Well, then I guess he must have turned himself invisible. That's what he invented, right?"

I groaned. Della's idea of what scientists do was based on the time she played Dr. Frankenstein in the fourth grade.

"People can't turn invisible," I said.

"But Dad said he was a scientist studying invisibility. What else would he be trying to do? He probably drank some chemicals that turned his body clear." She giggled. "Maybe he's running around the lab naked right now."

"He didn't turn himself clear," I said, rolling my eyes. "Besides, even if he did, clear isn't the same as invisible. You can still see things that are clear."

Della raised a disbelieving eyebrow at me.

"Glass is clear, but you can still see glass. It refracts light." I could feel my voice starting to rise. "If you really wanted to turn invisible, you'd have to figure out a way to stop light from touching you. Sure, maybe Dr. Learner can do that on a small scale, like molecular-level small, but there's no way he could invent something that could make him actually disappear. He'd have to change the laws of physics, and even then—"

I stopped mid-sentence when I noticed the smile on Della's face. She was winding me up.

"You're too easy, Alice!" Della laughed, and licked a bit of peanut butter off the side of her hand.

I put my face on the table and covered my head with my arms. I couldn't believe I fell for it. No one knew how to push my buttons like Della.

"That was payback for the milk shower you gave me before." Della paused. "But I still think his research must have had something to do with how he disappeared. I mean, he must have tons of gadgets and gizmos in his lab that he could use. Or some other scientist kidnapped him or something."

50

I wasn't a huge fan of the way Della used "gadgets and gizmos" to describe state-of-the-art scientific equipment, but she had a point. If anyone could figure out how to disable a security camera, it would be a scientist studying the physics of light.

"Well, as much as I'd love to sit and banter with you two sweethearts, I'm afraid I have a story to write," Dad said. "I'll leave you girls to clean up. I need to go do some research." He slurped down the last of his soup and kissed each of us on the forehead. Then he put his bowl in the sink, grabbed a water bottle out of the fridge, and went into his downstairs office.

"Story fever's setting in?" Della asked after the door shut.

The door swung open again and I jumped. Dad stuck his head out.

"Alice, we'll take a drive over to Delgado Industries in the morning and check things out, OK?"

He popped back into the office, closing the door behind him before I had a chance to answer.

"Oh, yeah. It's setting in big-time."

"I don't know how you live with him." She finished her toast and put her plate in the sink. I shrugged. I liked living with Dad. He let me do things my own way.

Della leaned against the wall and watched as I washed up. "So how do you fit into all this?" she asked.

"You remember that kid I texted you about? Sammy?"

"The one who follows you all over the school?"

51

I waited until she took the clean bowl I held out and started drying it before I answered her. "That's the one. Well, his father is Mr. Delgado."

"And he asked you to find the scientist?"

"That's about it."

Della tilted her head to the side. "Is he serious?"

I snorted. "No. He just wants me to run around and make a good story."

"And you said yes?"

I didn't answer, but I could feel my face starting to turn hot. I rinsed the last bowl and turned off the tap.

"Let me guess," Della said. "He made you angry and you took the case to prove him wrong." I blushed a little harder. We didn't live together anymore, but my sister could still read me like a book. Della handed me the dish towel. I guess I was finishing the drying too.

"I want to call Mom before I go to bed," she said in answer to my raised eyebrow.

I looked at the clock. "Della, it's after midnight in Italy right now. Mom's probably asleep."

Della let her shoulders slump tragically.

"Just call her when you wake up. She'll be having lunch when you have breakfast. It'll be like you're having brunch."

She seemed happy with that solution and made her way to

the stairs. Della put her foot on the first step and then turned around.

"You'll let me have the bed tonight, right? I need my REM sleep before an audition." She smiled sweetly.

I knew better than to argue. Arguing with Della was like arguing with a brick wall. You might make the best point in the world, but that wall wasn't budging for anyone.

"No problem."

Della walked upstairs belting out "Maybe." Her voice filled the house with an almost physical presence. I sighed. It looked like I'd be spending a lot of my summer vacation in the library. But then again, I would have done that anyway.

(7

I WOKE UP at 6:00 a.m. the next morning. The sun was shining, the birds were singing, and so was my sister.

"Good morning," Della trilled. She was working the top of her range, an octave usually reserved for calling dogs. Don't get me wrong, Della made it sound good. But I'd stayed up late going over the file Mr. Delgado had given me, and 6:00 a.m. is no time for music appreciation.

I sat up slowly, holding my head.

"Do you know what time it is?" I asked, not expecting an answer. The air bed had deflated slightly during the night and it was a struggle to free myself. The effort made me sweat, or maybe I was sweating already. Dad must not have turned on the air-conditioning. Either that or it was broken again. I hardly dared look at the thermometer. Another summer day in Philadelphia.

"I need a shower," I said, and stumbled out of the room.

"We need to leave by seven. I want to get to the theater early," Della called after me. I nodded, or said yes, I wasn't sure. I'm not what you'd call a morning person. The music scales started back up again behind me.

I turned on the shower and let the lukewarm water drown out the sound of singing and bring down my body temperature. Once I was more than half awake, I ran through what I'd read in the Delgado file.

Dr. Adrian Learner was seen going into his office after lunch on Wednesday, June 17. No one saw him again that day. When his assistant, Graham Davidson, came to check on him the next morning, the office was empty. When they reviewed the security footage, there were images of Dr. Learner entering his office, and then nothing. The door didn't open again until Davidson came. From the pictures of Dr. Learner's office and the basic floor plan Delgado had provided, it didn't look like there were any other ways out of that room. But I couldn't be sure until I'd seen it for myself. I was also looking forward to seeing the type of equipment Dr. Learner worked with. It might give me a clue about the type of invisibility he was studying. And maybe a clue to how he got past the security cameras too.

I had to admit, the Delgado case was starting to interest me. *The real question,* I thought, *is why did Dr. Learner disappear.*

Was he running away from something? Or had someone kidnapped him? He had looked pretty nervous in that security footage. I wondered what the equation was that would help me find the answer.

Della kicked the bathroom door for me to hurry up. I gave my hair one last rinse and turned off the water. I was dressed and ready to go in under ten minutes. We were in the car by 6:45 a.m. Dad pulled up at the corner of 9th and Walnut, right next to the theater. Even though the audition wasn't until 9:00 a.m., there was already a crowd. Girls of every shape and size stretched around the block, waiting for their chance to audition. There were a large number of redheads, not all natural. And next to them were the stage moms and dads polishing and primping their little stars.

Della climbed out of the car and smoothed her hair behind her ears.

"Break a leg, sweetie," Dad said. "Call me if you need anything."

I turned in my seat so I could wave to Della as we drove away. I don't know if she saw me or not, but she didn't wave back. She just squared her shoulders and took her place at the end of the line.

"Do you think she'll be OK?" I asked.

"What are you talking about? She'll be great. Your sister's a pro."

That wasn't what I meant. I was pretty sure Mom always went with Della to her auditions. But there was no point in making Dad worried now. Besides, Della knew what she was doing. She'd been on Broadway.

As we drove away from Center City, marble buildings turned to brick and then to sagging wood. The sidewalks became cracked and uneven, and the air streaming in through the Plymouth's open windows stank of old hot dogs and subway steam.

Then, as if someone had flipped a switch, we hit the suburbs. Like running into a green leafy wall, suddenly there were trees and grass and space between the houses.

Without any city traffic to hold him back, Dad hit the accelerator. It took Dad twenty minutes to get to the Delgado Industries building off Route 611. Legally, it should have taken forty. I just shut my eyes and counted the number of times we got honked at. Twenty-two. Not even close to the record.

Dad turned across traffic (twenty-three) and drove up between the two stone pillars that flanked the driveway. A large metal gate blocked us from driving any farther. In fact, the whole area around the building was fenced off. A surveillance camera pointed at the driver-side door. Dad leaned out of his open window and pressed the call button.

"Yes?" The voice was covered with static.

"Arthur Jones. *Philadelphia Daily News.*"

There was a long and official pause.

"I'm sorry, Mr. Jones. Your name isn't on the list."

I leaned across my father's lap and stuck my face in the camera. "Try *Alice* Jones," I said.

Another pause. And then without a word, the large gate swung open and we drove inside.

My father was quiet as we looked for a parking space. The kind of quiet a father gets when he's been shown up by his preteen daughter. But by the time he pulled into a spot near the door, he was over it. Nothing gets Dad down for long when he's on the trail of a good story. He climbed out of the car and whistled. "Now *that* is an office."

I had to agree. Delgado Industries was made of stone and ninety-degree angles. It looked like it had been designed on an Etch A Sketch. Maybe it wasn't everyone's style, but to me it was geometric perfection.

The doors to Delgado Industries were as large and imposing as the rest of the building. We waited for someone inside the complex to unlock the doors. There was a soft click and we pushed them open. Mr. Delgado ran a tight ship. I wondered how many different scientists worked there, and how many different experiments were going on at that very moment. For all I knew, someone was developing the next generation of superconductors less than a hundred feet away from where I stood. The thought made my skin tingle.

My dad and I stepped into a spacious vestibule, at least two stories high. Long rectangles of glass checkered the outer walls, sending stripes of early-morning sun across the floor. There were two silver elevators behind the main reception desk. They matched the silver flecks in the gray floor tiles. I bet someone did that on purpose. A hallway led out of the vestibule to my right, but it was blocked by waist-level turnstiles, the kind you get in subway and train stations but much more advanced. The busy hum of people filled the air. A lot of them wore lab coats, others suits, and there were a few in the unmistakable navy-blue uniforms of a private security firm, walkie-talkies strapped conspicuously to their utility belts. Everyone had a name badge.

Dad whistled again, craning his head back as we made our way to the reception desk.

"OK, Alice," he said. His nose twitched like he could physically sniff out the story. He checked that his notebook was in his pocket and his pencil was behind his ear. "Let me do the talking."

But Dad never got the chance. As we got to the desk, one of the silver elevators opened. Mr. Delgado's assistant, and possible android, stepped out to greet us.

"Ah, Alice. Mr. Delgado is so sorry he couldn't be here to meet you personally." He held out his hand. I shook it. He was one of those people who sandwiched your hand between his palms. I pulled back quickly and wiped my hand on the sides of my shirt. It looked like Dad and I were going to get special treatment. As far as Mr. Delgado was concerned, I was going to keep Delgado Industries on the front page of every newspaper in town. Mr. Delgado's assistant was there to make sure Dad and I only saw its good side.

"I'm Andrew, Mr. Delgado's Personal Secretary, and I will be supervising your tour of the facility." He put emphasis on the words *Personal* and *Secretary* as if they were capitalized like a royal title.

Dad cleared his throat.

"And Mr. Jones, so nice of you to join us too." Andrew turned his professional smile on my father. Then he stepped behind the reception desk, shooed the woman working there away from her computer, and began pressing buttons on the free keyboard.

I could sense the hostility coming off the shooed receptionist like some kind of force field. I actually felt a little bad for Andrew. No one likes it when you're better at their job than they are, but what was he supposed to do? Pretend to be stupid? A printer whirred and Andrew presented us with our ID badges. I was surprised to see the badges had our photos on them. One of the security cameras must have taken our pictures while Dad and I were waiting for someone to buzz us in. Next to the photo the words *One-Day Authorization* and the date were printed in big bold letters. Sammy wasn't kidding when he said his dad took security seriously.

"If you'll wear those and come with me, I will show you to Dr. Learner's lab."

We pinned on the badges and followed Andrew into the elevator. I could tell Dad was disappointed he wouldn't be able to use his pass to get back into the building later on, but he did his best to hide it. Andrew swiped his ID card and pressed the button for the first floor. I was surprised to see that we were going down.

"The building is built into the hillside," Andrew explained before I could ask. "Reception is at the top, all the labs are underneath. It makes the building very energy-efficient." Andrew launched into what sounded like a prepared speech about the merits of Delgado Industries' state-of-the-art building, timed perfectly to take us to the bottom floor.

The elevator doors behind us opened onto a long corridor. The wall in front of us, which ran along the length of the corridor, was glass. On the other side a long lawn, more manicured than a golf course, sloped away from the building until it reached a thick line of red maple trees.

Dad and Andrew started walking down the corridor, but I opened the file Mr. Delgado had given me and found the copy of the floor plan. Dr. Learner's lab took up most of the first floor. Only two of the other offices were labeled on the plan: A small space for Graham Davidson and a much larger office for Mr. Delgado. I would have thought Mr. Delgado's office would be somewhere on a top floor. But maybe he and Dr. Learner liked to be close to each other. They were old friends, after all.

There was a fire exit to the left of me, at the end of the corridor, but a large sign warned that opening the door would set off an alarm. I walked toward the wall and put my face against the glass, turning my head to the side. Judging from the seam where two panes connected, the windows were about two inches thick. I checked the edges. They were fixed in position. There was no way to open the window. Dr. Learner didn't get out that way either. I wiped my face print off the pristine pane with the sleeve of my shirt and ran to catch up with Andrew and my dad.

(8

IT WAS THE kind of place nightmares were made of, a long white hallway with endless identical doors and no way to tell them apart. Andrew appeared to be hesitating.

"I'm sure it was this one," he said, half under his breath. It was the first time I'd seen him less than 100 percent efficient. It made him seem almost human.

"What are we looking for?" I asked.

"Graham Davidson," Andrew said. He was the one in the security footage, I remembered. The one who discovered Dr. Learner was missing. "Mr. Delgado has ordered new nameplates for all of the doors, but there's been a delay. We were expecting them last week. Maintenance took off all the old nameplates, and then nothing." You could tell that Andrew was personally affronted by the inefficiency of the whole situation.

He took a breath and knocked on the door. If it was the wrong one, I wondered if he might self-destruct.

"What?" someone yelled from the other side. "It's open."

No sparks flew from Andrew's ears. I assumed we were speaking to the right man. Andrew opened the door.

Graham Davidson's office was slightly larger than a closet. His desk was wedged against the back wall, piled high with papers and books. There was one small space clear for his keyboard; everything else was chaos.

Graham Davidson sat hunched over his keyboard, copying data from a notebook into a large spreadsheet. He was built like an upside-down trapezoid. The way he hunched over made his nineteen-inch computer monitor look like a toy.

"Davidson. Alice Jones is here about Dr. Learner."

Dad cleared his throat.

"Excuse me. Alice Jones and her father, Arthur."

Graham didn't turn around. "Yes, yes, just let me finish this column."

"I was hoping you could accompany us to Dr. Learner's office and answer any of the more technical questions that they have."

Andrew waited for a response. All he got was the click of keys.

"Davidson?"

"There. Done." He snapped his notebook shut. "Yes, I'll

show your precious guests around. Data entry, group tours. I do have a PhD, you know."

Graham Davidson spun around in his chair and glared at us. He had the cap of a black ballpoint pen in the corner of his mouth. At least I think that's what it was. He'd chewed it to a pulp. I guess typing numbers into a computer wasn't Graham's idea of a fun time.

He pushed himself out of his chair and stalked down the corridor. "Follow me," he said without looking back.

Dad and Andrew were fine, but I had to jog to keep up.

"So, Andrew," Dad said, "where is Mr. Delgado today? I was hoping I could ask him a few more questions."

"Mr. Delgado is a very busy man." Andrew spoke with the pride of a father, even though Delgado must have been a good twenty years his senior. "He's at the University of Pennsylvania. He's the graduation speaker. They're awarding him an honorary doctorate." He paused for a moment, savoring the words.

"Honorary doctorate," Graham scoffed. "I spent eight years hunched over a microscope in a lab that smelled like wet towels before I got my degree. Not that it did me much good. Glorified errand boy. But donate a new science building and, hey presto, you're a doctor. Right, here we are."

He stopped in front of an industrial gray door and pulled a bunch of keys out of his lab-coat pocket. All the doors looked the same to me. I made a mental note that Dr. Learner's was the fifth door from the elevator, just in case I needed to find it again.

On the wall across from the one door to Dr. Learner's office, a small square surveillance camera pointed down at us. It was secured to the wall with an iron bracket and pointed directly at Dr. Learner's door.

"Is that the camera that recorded Dr. Learner's disappearance?" I asked.

Andrew flicked his eyes up over my shoulder, then looked back at me.

"Yes, that's the one. Aren't you clever?"

I couldn't tell if he was being sarcastic or serious, so I ignored him and took a closer look at the camera. It was fixed firmly in position, so no one could have adjusted the angle or tampered with where it was pointing. Besides, if anyone had moved the camera, we would have seen it on the recording.

I turned back to Graham as he found the right key and opened Dr. Learner's door.

"Who works in all of the other offices?" I asked.

"No one. The whole area past my office is Dr. Learner's. He needed more space, so they took out the walls between the offices and made it all one lab. And, before you ask, all the extra doors were sealed shut. There's no way you can open them."

Dr. Learner's office was a large rectangle, about four times as long as it was wide and crammed full of large metal machines.

The one closest to me looked like a giant telescope, but the label stuck to the side read A33ZX SERIES, BLUE ULTRON LASER. There were no beakers or test tubes or vials of strange-colored liquid, just wall-to-wall machines. I could almost feel the power coursing around the room.

Andrew stepped inside and stood with his back to the wall, like he was afraid he might break something. But that didn't bother Dad. He stalked around in his usual restless way, picking up anything that wasn't fixed to a table or too heavy to lift. Graham Davidson followed him, putting everything right with more than a little exasperation. Dad flicked a switch, and a large dangerous-looking piece of equipment started humming.

"So how long have you been Dr. Learner's assistant?" Dad asked.

"Mr. Delgado hired me about a year ago." Graham turned the switch back off quickly. "Dr. Learner was looking for someone to mentor, someone who would carry on his research once he retired. It was a dream job. I should have known it was too good to be true."

"That's a real shame." Dad shook his head. "What kind of research is it?"

"Physics."

Dad waited, but Graham didn't elaborate.

"What about you, Andrew? How long have you worked for Mr. Delgado?"

While Dad was keeping Graham and Andrew busy with easy questions, I moved to the far end of the office and started opening drawers and looking in cupboards, trying to find a clue as to what mysterious project Dr. Learner was working on.

I didn't get very far. All I could find were small metal tubes, wires, little mirrors, and a shelf full of protective gloves and goggles.

I was just about to give up when I saw something at the back of a metal cabinet. A square of blackness that was just a little bit darker than the rest. I reached in and pulled out a box covered in soft black velvet.

I opened the lid.

The inside of the box was covered in black velvet too, and a small flap of the fabric lay loose across the bottom. I lifted it and gasped. There, lying on top of the cloth, were ten of the biggest diamonds I'd ever seen.

"What are you doing?" Graham demanded. He took a pair of tongs carefully out of my father's hands. "This lab is full of precision equipment. Andrew, watch him. Make sure he doesn't touch anything else."

Graham came across the office to me. He held out his hand, and I put the box in it.

"Are those real diamonds?" I asked.

Graham glared at me. "They're industrial. They're for the lasers, not jewelry."

He opened the box and counted the jewels, like I'd be dumb enough to steal something with everyone watching me. Besides, I'm not exactly a diamond-necklace type of girl. I'd rather have a new scientific calculator.

"Do they make the laser more accurate?"

Graham looked at me like I'd said something incredible. "Not exactly, but you're close. They increase efficiency and make the laser stronger. You can do a lot more with less power."

I looked over his shoulder. Andrew was watching us suspiciously, and my dad was messing around with some papers next to Dr. Learner's computer.

"Can you show me?" It was the first solid clue about the nature of Dr. Learner's research. But I also wanted to see how it worked.

Graham grumbled, but it wasn't his best effort. I could tell he wanted to play with the lasers as much as I did.

"Well," he said after a minute, "I guess I could show you *some* of the equipment."

He opened the side panel of one of the smaller machines that looked like a mini-fridge with a missing door. Graham fit one of the diamonds inside and closed the panel.

"What do you think you're doing?" Andrew appeared behind Graham's shoulder. He didn't look happy.

"Keep your shirt on. I'm just showing her how the

invisibility cube works: It isn't top secret. You can see videos on YouTube."

Graham got four pairs of safety glasses off the shelf and handed us each a pair.

"I need something small. This only works on a very small scale." He patted his pockets like an old man looking for his keys. "Ah." He smiled, then took the ruined top off the pen in his pocket and put it inside the box. "Are you ready?"

I put on the glasses and nodded.

Graham flipped the switch. The machine started to hum and the cap was gone. Instantly, like it had disappeared off the face of the earth.

"Wow." It was all I could say. It was still only invisibility on a small scale, but it was a lot bigger than I thought was possible. Maybe Sammy hadn't been exaggerating about how smart Dr. Learner was after all.

"Touch it." Davidson nudged my shoulder.

I reached out my finger toward where I'd last seen the cap. I could feel it. It was still right there inside the cube. But I couldn't see it. I couldn't see the tip of my finger either.

We see things because light bounces off them and back into our eyeballs, which is why you can't see in the dark. No light, no sight. Normally, light moves in a straight line, but Dr. Learner's machine must have been bending the light around the pen cap. It was making it invisible. It was so cool

I didn't even care that I was touching something that had been in Graham Davidson's mouth.

"Is this related to the breakthrough Dr. Learner had?" I asked. "Was he trying to make this work on a larger scale?"

"What?" Graham turned off the machine and the black cap popped back into view.

"Mr. Delgado said Dr. Learner had a breakthrough. He had a press conference yesterday to unveil the results. Well, he would have if Dr. Learner hadn't gone missing."

"A breakthrough?" Graham looked confused. "Not that I knew about, not that Dr. Learner would share any of his important research with me. Oh, no. I don't know why he wanted a lab assistant in the first place, unless it was to have someone to get him coffee. He never had any appreciation of my skills. He never even let me babysit experiments for him. He'd be here all hours of the night because he couldn't bear to leave an experiment unfinished, and he refused to let me help. And that was *before* he got super-paranoid."

"Wait." I held up a hand to stop Graham's rant. "Did something specific happen to spook Dr. Learner?"

"It wasn't anything I did, if that's what you're implying." Graham searched me for an accusation. "But maybe you're right. He did get a lot worse about six months ago. He even started taking his notes home in a locked briefcase every night." Graham trailed off as if he'd thought of something important.

71

"What is it?" I asked.

Graham shook himself. "What? Oh, nothing. I just remembered I have to do something. Are you just about done here?"

I wanted to ask what Graham had remembered. I was pretty sure it had something to do with that briefcase, and I wanted to know what it was. Maybe Dr. Learner had figured out how to make the invisibility cube work for larger objects. But Andrew butted in first.

"Yes, I think we're just about finished here." He looked at his watch. "I need to go collect Mr. Delgado from the unive—Mr. Jones!" Andrew spoke sharply, and my dad quickly put down a small soldering iron.

Andrew took a calming breath and herded us all out of the room. Graham Davidson left too, locking the door behind him. I wondered if he was allowed to go into Dr. Learner's lab without supervision. If it was me, I'd spend all day playing with that invisibility cube. But I guess the security camera meant he couldn't sneak in, even if he did have the key.

I looked at the camera one more time as we walked past. Something about it bugged me, but I couldn't figure out what. I wanted to stop and take a closer look, but Andrew must have been in a real hurry to fetch Mr. Delgado. He was already at the end of the hall, tapping his foot like that would make me move faster. I took a quick picture so I could look at it later, and then I ran the rest of the way down the hall.

(9

I CLIMBED INTO the car and slammed the door behind me.

Dad slid behind the steering wheel, grinning like a kid in a candy store. "What a scoop!"

I was only half listening. I'd figured out why the security camera was bothering me. It was too small.

I pulled out the photos from the file Delgado had given me. There. In one of the shots taken from inside Dr. Learner's lab, you could see the security camera through the open office door. I took out my phone and looked at the picture I'd just taken.

In the picture from the Delgado file, there was an L-shaped bracket hooked to the side of the camera. Two small clips came out of the foot of the L. They looked like they were designed to hold something flat. Maybe a mirror to see around corners, or something to block out glare if the camera was near a window.

But the camera outside Dr. Learner's office wasn't near a corner or a window. So what was the bracket for? And since there was no bracket on the security camera when we were in the office today, where had it gone?

"Alice, didn't you hear me? I said, what a scoop!"

The car shuddered to life, coughing up black smoke as we pulled out of the Delgado Industries parking lot and back onto the road. Dad is a reckless driver, so I expected to hear at least a couple of horns sound off as he pulled into traffic without slowing down. The silence was so unexpected, it made me turn around. A silver Mercedes with a New York license plate was right behind us. *It must be a rental,* I thought. Either that or their horn was broken. There was no way a real New York driver would let Dad get away with cutting them off like that.

"This story has everything!" Dad changed lanes to pass someone doing the speed limit. "We already had a mysterious disappearance and some sort of top-secret invisibility project. Now we've got a forty-million-dollar government contract, possible corporate espionage, and—best of all—that invisibility project? It was a suit! Dr. Learner was working on an invisibility *suit*!"

"Wait, how do you know all that?"

"Ah, well, I may have taken a little peek at Dr. Learner's computer while you three were messing around with that machine. Nice work, by the way." Dad took a sharp corner without signaling and kept talking over the blaring horns.

"How did you even get into his computer? Didn't he have a password?"

"Yes, well, fortunately for me, Dr. Learner was the forgetful type. He wrote all his passwords down on a handy little Post-it and stuck it under his keyboard. His computer is about as secure as a brown paper bag."

"So what did you find?"

"A ton of emails from Mr. Delgado asking Dr. Learner to get 'all the data about the suit' ready for an important meeting. There was also an email offering Dr. Learner a new job."

"So he was definitely working on a suit?"

"That's what the emails said."

"But that's not possible."

"I'm telling you, it was right there in the emails."

"And I'm telling *you* there's no way an invisibility suit could be real."

Scientists have been trying to figure out a way to make people invisible for years. The closest they've come is using cameras to take photos of whatever is behind the suit and projecting it on the front of the suit, but that isn't really invisibility. That's more like a chameleon changing color to match its surroundings. Plus there are always problems with camera delay.

But the kind of suit Dad was talking about—one that could actually bend light—no one had even come close.

"Why can't it be real? What about that invisibility cube the lab assistant showed you? That looked real enough to me."

"That's different," I said. "The pen cap had to be inside the box to disappear. If you used that technology to make a person invisible, he'd have to stand still inside something the size of a refrigerator. And you heard how much noise it made. What's the use of being invisible if people can hear you coming from a mile away?"

Dad laughed. "OK, OK. So maybe it isn't a suit *yet*. Maybe they're still trying to figure it out. Maybe Dr. Learner has invented a way to make pen caps invisible outside of the box? Have you thought about that?"

I started to tell Dad he was being worse than Della, but stopped. If you'd told me before breakfast I would see a pen cap vanish before my eyes, I never would have believed you.

"Maybe," I said slowly, drawing out the word. If Dr. Learner had made that kind of breakthrough, it was no wonder Mr. Delgado wanted him and his research back. It would be priceless.

Dad banged his hands triumphantly on the steering wheel.

"But just because it's possible doesn't mean it's true," I said quickly. I didn't want Dad to get carried away.

"It doesn't mean it's not true either."

Dad's phone bleeped, saving me from any more of his crowing. He shifted in his seat so I could pull it out of his back pocket.

"Seriously?" I asked.

"It could be important."

I rolled my eyes and got the phone with as little butt contact as possible.

"It's from Della. The audition is running late. She wants you to bring her some lunch."

"No problem," Dad said, so I sent Della the good news. I put the phone in the cup holder on the dashboard, just in case anyone else called.

"So, Dr. Learner had another job offer?" I said. Dad nodded. It made sense. If there were even hints that Dr. Learner's research might make a real invisibility suit possible, everyone would want him to work for them. And if he didn't come willingly, they might even take him by force.

"What was the name of the company?" I asked.

"Chronos R & D."

I'd have to look them up.

We stopped at Logan Square, double-parking outside the Franklin Institute, the greatest science museum in the world. Dad gave me a twenty and I ran across the street to get in line at one of the small metal food carts in front of the museum. The banner hanging from a lamppost showed an impossible staircase:

Math and the Art of M. C. Escher. Tickets were probably expensive, but maybe I could talk Dad into taking me when this Delgado business was over. We used to love going to the Franklin Institute. It was one of the few outings that the whole family enjoyed.

The man in front of me finished paying and took his food and the smell of fried onions with him.

"Three soft pretzels with mustard, two cherry Cokes, and a Sprite," I ordered quickly, craning my neck to check on Dad to make sure a traffic cop hadn't forced him to move the car.

The Plymouth was still there. I gave a little sigh of relief and stopped halfway. The silver Mercedes was there too, waiting patiently behind my dad instead of trying to go around. Other drivers honked angrily as they forced their way past both cars. I felt a small shiver, but brushed it away. The driver was probably from out of town. Somewhere small and polite where you didn't drive on the wrong side of the road no matter what.

The vendor handed me three piping-hot brown paper bags and three cans of soda, and I struggled not to drop them all as I jogged back to where Dad was blocking traffic. On my way, I took a look inside the Mercedes. There were two men sitting in the front. They looked perfectly normal, and I felt foolish for being suspicious.

"Here." I leaned in through the window and handed Dad his and Della's share of the food. He needed to go to the office to pitch his story, and it was quicker for me to walk home from the museum rather than from the Walnut Street Theatre.

"I'll see you back at the house," Dad said, and swerved out into the traffic.

I watched Dad drive down Race Street. The silver Mercedes was right behind him. For some reason they didn't look like tourists anymore. I felt a cold knot twist in the pit of my stomach. I grabbed my phone and snapped a picture right before the car turned onto 21st Street. The same direction my dad had gone. I was getting ready to dial 911 when I noticed the next three cars turning in the same direction. There was roadwork at the end of the street. All the cars were turning that way. This Delgado case was making me jumpy.

I shook myself and started the walk home, counting my steps as I went. The city smelled of summer—hot concrete and the things that stuck to it. I took a swig of my cherry cola and tried to shake off my gloom. I knew what the problem was. The case was too important. I'd lost track of how many mysteries I'd solved for people at school. But finding the basketball team's missing bake sale money was one thing. Finding a missing scientist working on a top-secret invisibility project . . . that was a whole new level.

I took a breath and thought about math. Even the most complicated equations can be simplified. I just needed to look at all the factors and break them down. According to the security camera, Dr. Learner hadn't left his office. That meant there were four possibilities. One: There was another exit from Dr. Learner's office. Two: Someone had tampered with the security camera. Three: Dr. Learner was still in his office now. Four: Dr. Learner was invisible.

I laughed to myself. As impressive as Graham Davidson's demonstration had been, I just couldn't believe Dr. Learner had made a working invisibility suit. A breakthrough in the right direction, maybe, but not a working suit. I like to see things before I believe them. Although I had to wonder, could you *see* an invisibility suit or was it invisible? I laughed a little louder, and a man screaming into his cell phone stared at me like I was crazy. I ignored him and kept walking.

It took about twenty minutes to get home. The pale strip of skin where I parted my hair burned, and I knew brushing it later would be like holding a match to my scalp. My shirt clung to the small of my back. It might as well have been raining. I gave a sigh of relief when I saw our front steps. And then I sighed again. Sammy Delgado Jr. was sitting on them.

"Alice!" he shouted, jumping up. He was wearing pressed tan shorts, a blue button-down shirt, and a navy-blue blazer. He looked like something out of a sailing magazine. "Hi. I was waiting for you. We didn't get to talk yesterday." Sammy blushed and looked at his shoes. He was probably remembering that the last time I saw him he was running out of a room in tears.

"Hi, Sammy." I stepped past him and unlocked the front door. Sammy stood on the top step watching me, the way a dog watches you when you're making a sandwich.

"Would you like to come in?" I asked. I didn't have much of a choice.

It was like I'd offered him a ticket to Disney World. He bounded in and then stood there, unsure of what to do next.

"Sit down," I said, nodding toward the couch on the living-room side of things. "I'll get us a drink. What do you want?" I opened the fridge and stood staring at the practically empty shelves, trying to soak up the coolness. "We have water."

I needed to remind Dad to go shopping.

"Water's good," Sammy answered.

"So why are you here?" I put some ice cubes in a glass, filled it from the tap, and handed it to Sammy.

"I'm here to talk about the case! I wanted to come this morning, but Dad made me go to the university and watch him graduate." Sammy flopped down onto the couch. "So what did you find at the lab? Were there any clues? Did anyone act suspicious?"

"I told you. I don't need a partner."

"I know, but you're working for my dad."

"So I need to let you tag along?"

"No, but I want to help. I really like Dr. Learner. I want to help find him. It's important." Sammy stuck out his chin. He

81

put it back when he saw me staring. "I know Dr. Learner. I know all sorts of things about him. I have inside information."

It was like fending off a dog with a stick. He just kept coming back for more. "Well, do you know where Dr. Learner is?" I asked.

Sammy was silent. He looked miserable. I sighed again. I was starting to hate myself a little bit. Like my dad said, I should give Sammy a break.

"All right. I get it. You just want to help. So, what can you tell me about Dr. Learner?"

"Well, he's great. He's super-smart, but a little bit weird. But I guess a lot of smart people are weird. Not that I'm saying *you're* weird, Alice."

"Whoa, Sammy, slow down. Just tell me what you know."

Sammy took a gulp of water, coughed as it went down the wrong way, and then tried again. "Dr. Learner's really nice. He lets me watch his experiments, even the dangerous ones. And he'll always explain the things I don't understand. He's great at explaining things. But he's been different ever since Christmas. It's like he's always thinking about something else."

That was about the same time Graham Davidson said Dr. Learner started to get secretive. And when Mr. Delgado said he had his big breakthrough. I guess he was worried about the competition trying to steal his ideas too. I wondered if he worried about being kidnapped.

"How was he different? Did something happen?"

Sammy shifted uncomfortably in his seat and looked at his shoes like they were the most fascinating things in the room.

"Was he having trouble at work?" I tried again. "Was there a reason he'd want to run away?"

Still no response.

"Sammy?" I said it more sharply than I meant to, and Sammy jumped.

"No," he said sheepishly. "I don't know about any trouble."

"Well, what about his invisibility research? You said you helped him. Can you tell me exactly what he was working on? Do you have any idea where it is?"

Sammy jumped again, his mouth open in a perfect O. I guess he'd forgotten he told me that.

"I did help him," Sammy said slowly, sitting on his hands to stop them from twitching. "But not in the lab. I mean I could have, I'm pretty good at science, but Dad doesn't like it when I visit the labs. He says I'm a nuisance." He paused just long enough to take a breath and kept talking. "But I helped Dr. Learner in a lot of other ways, like running errands and tidying up for him. Things like that." He trailed off.

I didn't buy it. No one brags that they helped the guy accepting the award by keeping his room clean. And Sammy *did* say he'd helped in the lab before. Then again, this was Sammy. What did I know?

"So he was just different. Maybe he was just busy?"

Sammy bit his lip and shook his head. "No, he wasn't just busy. He was different. He'd forget to do the things he promised. He never used to do that. I think he must have been in serious trouble. And now he's missing. And all his research too. You need to find him, Alice."

Sammy looked at me with big wet eyes, like somehow I was going to make everything all better. But this wasn't a squirrel hiding in a secret passageway; this was a real missing person.

"Tell me about how your dad and Dr. Learner met." I didn't think it was important; I just wanted to change the subject.

"Well, I think they met when they were in graduate school at the University of Pennsylvania. They were in the Physics Department. My dad donated money for a whole new science building, you know."

"So I heard," I said.

"They were always putting on shows together. Dad told me, this one time—"

I interrupted him. "Keep to the point, Sammy."

"Yeah, anyway, Dr. Learner got some big prize and went to work at a lab somewhere in California, and when Dad opened his own company he hired Dr. Learner to come back to Pennsylvania and work for him. Dad says they always dreamed of opening a science company together."

Sammy wiped his nose with the back of his arm. He looked

at me expectantly, like he'd just given me all the clues I could possibly need and all he had to do was sit back and let me solve the mystery.

I took the empty glass out of Sammy's hand. "OK, Sammy. Thanks for your help."

"Wait, is that it?"

"That's it." I knew I was letting him down, but it wasn't my fault Sammy thought I was some kind of hero.

"But what about the lab? Don't you want to talk about what you found out there? Shouldn't we start chasing down leads?"

The questions rained down with no signs of letting up. And then I had a flash of inspiration.

When I was younger and asking my father endless questions, he used to send me on a treasure hunt. First he'd ask for something easy, like a white pillow or an apple. And then something harder and harder until he asked for the impossible, and I was too into the game to stop looking. I remember one time he asked for a rainbow frog. I searched the park for three hours before my mother came and found me.

"Actually, there is something you could help me with," I said. Sammy's face lit up like the Fourth of July.

"What? What can I do?"

"I know you're not supposed to, but can you get into your dad's lab?" I asked.

Sammy grinned. "Sure, I go there all the time. But don't tell my dad, OK?"

"OK, I won't," I agreed. I took out the photos of Dr. Learner's office. "Here. Look at this. Can you see the surveillance camera?"

Sammy nodded.

"Can you see this metal piece clipped to the side?"

He nodded again, so hard I worried he might shake his brain loose.

"Is it a clue? Is that how Dr. Learner got out of the office?" Sammy spoke excitedly, barely finishing one question before asking another. "What do you think it is? Some sort of jamming device? Like for radar? Or a hologram projector? Or—"

I stopped him before he bit his tongue.

"I don't know what it is," I said mysteriously. "But when I was there today, it was gone. I don't know if it's important or not, but if you could find that piece of metal it might be a big help."

Sammy's eyes sparkled. His mouth opened and then closed and then opened again.

"But make sure you don't let people know you're looking for it. If it *is* connected to all this, then it might be dangerous." I couldn't resist making the job seem more important than it was. With any luck, Sammy would be out of my hair and searching for that metal "rainbow frog" for the rest of the summer.

(10

ONCE I GOT Sammy out of the house, I shut myself in Dad's office. I wanted to look up the name of the company that had been emailing Dr. Learner. It was the only solid lead I had.

Chronos R & D. The R & D stood for Research and Development, apparently.

They were based in upstate New York. Really upstate, where there are forests and farms and it snows in feet not inches. Their website said they were "an independent research facility working with the world's top scientists to solve the world's top problems."

The Google news feed said they weren't very nice.

I found three lawsuits against Chronos R & D, and that was just on the first page. The lawsuits were still ongoing, so no details were published, but from what I could see, Chronos was accused of misappropriating research. Which is a fancy way of saying they stole it. Chronos would find out what project a competing company was working on and then they'd start working on the same thing. And they'd usually get results first. If they were doing all the work on their own, well, there was nothing you could do about it. But if they were getting ahead by "peeking" at the other research first? Then they were in big trouble.

If Chronos R & D was emailing Dr. Learner, did that mean they were after his research? Did they really want him to work for them, or did they just need to get close enough to steal his results? Dr. Learner's invisibility suit would have to be pretty amazing if they were willing to take that kind of risk. If they got caught there'd be huge fines. They might even end up in jail. Dr. Learner and Mr. Delgado were friends, so I didn't think Dr. Learner would leave and take his invisibility suit to another company. Still, it was hard to tell what people would do for the right amount of money. I should know. I once saw a kid eat a worm for ten dollars.

I should have asked how much those diamonds in Dr. Learner's office were worth. Graham Davidson said they were industrial, but they were still diamonds. It made me wonder if the ten I saw were the only ones there.

The front door slammed.

I turned off the computer and followed the sound of chaos. Della thundered past me and ran up the stairs, her arms full of sheet music. I heard my bedroom door slam, then open again. Dad came in behind her. He looked a bit like he'd been hit by a cement mixer.

"What's going on?" I asked.

"Della got a callback. They want to see her again. She's trying to decide if she should dye her hair."

"A callback is good news, isn't it? Why does she look so upset?"

Della came back downstairs, looking around like she'd forgotten something.

"All the other girls who got called back have red hair," she said. "I want them to know I'm committed, but I don't want them to think that I'm . . ."

"Desperate," I finished her sentence.

Della looked hurt.

"I don't mean you are desperate, I just mean it would *look* like it if you went and dyed your hair for a callback." I'm no good at pep talks. I tend to say the first thing that comes to mind. And apparently, the first things that come into my mind aren't very tactful. I wondered if Della was always like this at auditions, or if it was just because Mom wasn't there to hold her hand.

"Well, to be honest, I am a little desperate. I'm twelve. It's probably the last year I can play Annie."

"But you're a young twelve," Dad said soothingly. "You could pass for ten."

Della must be the only twelve-year-old in the world who was happy to be told she looks younger. But Annie was a dream role, even *I* knew that much.

"I think you should stay blonde," Dad said. "If everyone else has red hair, it will make you stand out more. You can always dye it later if they want."

"I think so too," I said quickly.

Della tilted her head to one side, to emphasize the fact that she was thinking it over.

Dad snuck a look at his watch. It was two in the afternoon, which meant he had five hours before they put the paper to bed. He was probably worried about getting his follow-up story on Dr. Learner's disappearance finished on time.

It didn't look like Della was going to make up her mind any time soon.

"Why don't you call Mom?" I asked. "It's around dinnertime in Italy now. It's the perfect time to talk."

Della hit me with her megawatt smile. "You're a genius, Alice! I'll be upstairs. Don't interrupt me until dinner. We'll be dancing at the callback, so I'll need something carb heavy. Pasta, around six." And with that she turned around and went back upstairs.

Dad lifted his glasses and massaged the bridge of his nose. "And now that that crisis is over, I need to get back to the office."

"Did they approve your story?"

"Not exactly," he sighed. "A corporate espionage story has to be vetted by the legal team. There's no way they could do that in time." Dad walked over to the fridge and got himself a fresh water bottle. "The editor said I could keep working on it, but he needs something to fill the news hole for tomorrow. So now I have until the end of today to write a heartwarming tale of a man doing whatever it takes to find his friend."

Puff pieces always made Dad cranky. They didn't fit his Arthur Jones, Crusader for Truth persona. Plus, we both knew Mr. Delgado was anything but heartwarming.

"I'm sorry, Dad," I said. "Is there anything I can do to help?"

I saw the trap as soon as the words were out of my mouth, but it was already too late.

"I'm so glad you asked. Yes, Alice, there *is* something you can do. I need you to get down to Dr. Learner's apartment and interview his neighbors. Get me some background details, you know, sniff out a personal angle."

Overhead, Della started tap dancing. I think she was showing Mom her kick ball change. It sounded like a million angry neighbors pounding on the ceiling. Or maybe that was me having a premonition. Dad took my momentary distraction as a chance to make his escape out of the front door. I only just managed to catch up with him.

"Are you serious? You want me to go to Learner's apartment building alone and interview the neighbors? What do you think I'm going to find?"

Graham Davidson's voice popped into my head: *He even started taking his notes home in a locked briefcase every night.*

"Do you think I'll find Dr. Learner's top-secret research? Wouldn't the police have searched his apartment already?"

"Dr. Learner's only been missing for twenty-four hours. There's no way the police have been to his place yet. At least not to do more than check and see that he's really missing. Go on, have a look. Maybe you'll get lucky." Dad smiled. "Just get me something sympathetic. Who was the man behind the scientist? That sort of thing. The neighbors will open up to you. No one wants to tell things to a reporter. It makes them feel bad."

He climbed into the Plymouth and started the engine.

I ran down the steps and stood in front of the car with my hands on the hood, blocking him in.

I wanted to ask him why he didn't get Della to go do his interviews; she is way more likable than I am. But I didn't. I knew why Dad asked me. We were a team. We had been since the day I came back to live with him in Philadelphia.

"Come on, Alice, we're on a deadline. If you're worried about going alone, call a friend." Dad leaned out of the window and wiggled his eyebrows at me.

"Don't be ridiculous. Who's going to go on such a crazy errand?" I asked. "And don't say Sammy. I just got rid of him."

I could tell Dad wasn't going to give up. When there was a story at stake, he was a man on a mission. I had about thirty seconds before he'd start nudging me with the front bumper to get me out of the way. But just because I was going to help him didn't mean I had to make it easy.

"All right," I said. "I'll do your background research for you. But I want something in return."

"Name it."

"The killer Sudoku puzzle in the paper is mine for the rest of the summer. And the cryptic quip. I get to do the whole thing, and I don't want you peeking over my shoulder making suggestions."

Dad looked appalled, like I'd asked him to give me a kidney. "How about a month?"

I bent forward and stared him down through the windshield. "The rest of the summer, take it or leave it."

"You drive a hard bargain, Alice." He sucked on his teeth. I couldn't believe he had to think about it. "OK, fine," he said. "It's yours, but I want detailed notes and photographs of the scene."

"Deal." I stepped back onto the sidewalk, and Dad cranked the wheel and started to drive away. He slammed on the brakes while he was still halfway in the parking spot and leaned out of the window again.

"Find out if he has a cat. People love a pet angle."

And then he hit the accelerator and disappeared up the road.

(11

DAD HAD FIVE hours before his story was due. And I had four before Della needed me to make dinner. There was no time to waste. I took the stairs up to my bedroom two at a time.

"Della, I'm going out. I'll be back in time to make dinner." That's what I was *going* to say, anyway. But I didn't get the chance.

When I opened the door, Della had her back to me, but I could tell from the hunch of her shoulders that she was upset.

"I know, Mom," she said. "But it's really hard. Dad and Alice don't understand. And Dad's working on a story . . ."

I took a step back and shut the door as quietly as I could. The floorboard under my left foot creaked. I froze, but Della didn't seem to notice.

"I'm fine," she said. "Alice is cooking dinner tonight. Yes, I told her, carbs."

It made me roll my eyes and smile at the same time. Even when she was upset, my sister was serious about being an actress.

"I don't know. I don't think she minds. But it's weird. He's supposed to be the one taking care of us, not the other way around."

It felt like I'd been kicked. Della went quiet. I could imagine Mom on the other end of the line, somewhere in a fancy hotel in Italy, saying comforting things. They must have worked. Della gave a kind of *let's put all of this behind us* sigh.

"You're right, I should just focus on the callback. Will you listen to my routine again?"

I used the cover of Della's time step to sneak down the stairs. I scribbled a note and left it on the kitchen counter before grabbing my bike and heading out of the door.

It was just after a quarter past one and the bright, sharp heat of mid-afternoon was fading into a thick mugginess that radiated off the sides of buildings and sunbaked streets and would last long after nightfall. I rode on the sidewalk even though you aren't supposed to. There weren't many people around, and it seemed a lot safer than being on the street.

I couldn't believe Della was being such a drama queen. Then again, it was Della. Drama was what she did best. I pedaled hard and wished I hadn't gone upstairs in the first place. Then I wouldn't be back stuck in the middle of Mom and Dad, the absolute worst place in the world. It was like I was eight all over again, telling Mom I wanted to go back to Philly to live with Dad. My palms were sweating just remembering it.

I took a breath and tried to pretend the whole thing away. Della didn't know I'd heard her, so as far as I was concerned, it never happened. I was never choosing sides again.

"Numbers! Hey, what's up?"

Kevin Jordan came flying out of an alley on the other side of the street. I slammed hard on the brakes. My stomach flipped so impressively it could have run away to join the circus.

"What do you want?" I asked.

"What? Nothing." He checked the road quickly and cycled across when traffic was clear. "Your dad just called me. He said you were going to some guy's apartment, and he couldn't go with you so he asked me."

My father. The Hero. I planned to kill him when I got home.

I stood still, one foot on the ground, the other perched on the pedal. The boy was like a bad penny. Kevin circled his bike around me.

"What exactly do you think you're doing?" I asked.

"I just said, your dad asked me—"

"Yes"—I cut him off—"but what do you think *you're* doing?

We aren't exactly friends. Don't you have something better to do with your summer than hassle me?"

"Hey, I'm here to help. No need to get so hostile. Besides, you owe me. I skipped out on Principal Chase to try to save you from those guys yesterday. Even though I knew she'd give me summer detention. I'm your hero."

Kevin screwed up his angel face and stared at his shoes. It looked like I was bullying a choirboy. An old lady walking her Maltese gave me a look so dirty you'd think I just crawled out of a sewer grate. A nicer person might have felt bad about that. Not me.

"No need to be hostile? Look, Kevin, I don't like you. And you don't like me, so why . . ." I trailed off. "My dad said he'd pay you, didn't he?"

"Twenty bucks." Kevin grinned so wide I could see he'd forgotten to brush his teeth that morning.

"Do what you like," I said.

Dr. Learner lived in the Drake Towers, a small apartment complex next to the Delaware River. We pulled into the parking lot at the front and locked our bikes to the chain-link fence. The building was made out of concrete, three stories of pale gray that cut into the skyline like a chisel. An open walkway ran along the second and third floors, so all of the apartments had their own outside door. It looked more like a motel than a place someone would live full-time. It seemed odd that Mr. Delgado lived in a mansion while his close friend lived in a place like this, but I guess that's the difference between owning a business and working for one.

Dr. Learner lived in apartment 203, so I skipped the doors on the ground floor and headed straight for the steps. Kevin jogged behind me.

"So, are we just going to knock on the doors and ask people questions?"

"Pretty much."

I stopped in front of the first door and raised my hand to knock. Then I stopped and turned to face Kevin. He was grinning like an idiot and making me more than a little nervous.

"Look," I said. "This is for my dad's work. So try to act normal, OK?"

Kevin crossed his heart and hoped to die. The grin didn't go away. I shook my head. I bet Dad had made this sound really exciting over the phone.

"And let me do the talking," I said.

No one was home at 200. Or at 201. Or, if they were home, they were ignoring me.

I was just starting to think I might get lucky and not have to talk to anyone when I knocked on the door of 202. Whoever lived there must have heard me knocking on the other doors, because they were ready for me.

As soon as my knuckles brushed the wood, the door jerked open so hard it rattled the security chain.

"What do you want?"

The woman on the other side of the door eyed us like we might be wanted criminals. She was wearing a powder-blue sweat suit, and her hair was dyed the color of a dull penny. She was due for a touch-up. I could see a line of gray at her roots. I made a mental note to tell Della she should definitely stay blonde.

"Uh, hi," I said. "My name is Alice and this is Kevin. We just wanted to ask some questions about Dr. Learner. He lives in apartment 203."

The woman narrowed her eyes.

"He's my uncle. He's gone missing, and we're looking for him," Kevin said, polishing up his halo.

I elbowed Kevin hard. What part of "Let me do the talking" didn't he understand?

"I don't know what your game is, little missy, but I ain't playing. And you"—she sniffed at Kevin—"that pretty face doesn't fool me for one second. If you think you're gonna smile my door open and steal my jewelry, you picked the wrong old lady to mess with."

"Honestly," I said. "We just want to talk."

She snorted. "If you want someone to talk, try ol' jabber-jaws in 206. That woman could talk the hind legs off a donkey.

Now back up and back off!" And with that, she slammed the door.

I should have asked for more than just the Sudoku puzzle and the cryptic quip.

"Wow," Kevin said.

"Come on, let's try the rest of them." I walked past Dr. Learner's apartment and knocked on the door to 204. No answer.

"She was crazy." Kevin followed me down the walkway to 205. He might have had a point, but I wasn't about to admit it.

"Why? Because she didn't buy your angel face?"

"No. Because she was crazy." Kevin crossed his arms and leaned against the concrete wall while we waited to see if anyone would answer. "What are you trying to find out anyway? Do you think one of these people will know where he is?"

"Not really," I said. We walked down to the next door. "I'm just doing my dad a favor." I knocked on 206. The sooner I could find some background information and get out of there the better.

This time the door opened.

An elderly woman in a flowery tropical dress smiled out at us. She was almost my height, with dark skin that wrinkled happily around her eyes and short, curly gray hair.

"Hello there. Can I help you?" A small Pomeranian yipped at us from behind her legs. "Quiet, Betsy!"

"My name is Alice and this is Kevin. We wanted to ask you some questions about Dr. Learner from 203."

"Come in, come in," she said, and shooed us into the living room. Betsy ran circles around her legs. The furniture was as floral as her dress. Small porcelain figures of dogs dressed up as flowers filled the shelves.

"Please, sit down. It's so nice to have company. I just baked some cookies. My grandson loves these, but I can always bake some more for when he comes over later." She put a plate full of chocolate-chip cookies on the coffee table in front of us, then settled herself down. "Now, what did you two dears want to talk about?"

"Well, Mrs., um?" I started, picking up a cookie from the plate to be polite.

"Call me Dot, dear. Everyone calls me Dot."

"OK, Dot. We wanted to ask you about Dr. Learner. Your neighbor in 203."

"Oh, Adrian, such a charming man. He always used to bring me my mail. So helpful, although, well, it hardly matters I suppose . . ."

"What is it?"

"Well, one doesn't like to speak ill of the dead . . ."

"He isn't dead," I said quickly. "He's just missing."

"Oh, well, that's good, then. Would you like another

cookie?" I hadn't finished the one in my hand, but Kevin had already eaten three and reached out for another.

"No, thank you." I shot Kevin a disapproving look, which he expertly ignored. "What were you going to say about Dr. Learner?"

"Hmm?"

It was like watching molasses roll uphill.

"Dr. Learner. Something was different? You noticed something?"

"Oh, that. Well, I'm not one to tell tales. And I do think he must have been very busy, so I'm sure it isn't all his fault. But, well, busy or not, you do need to have some consideration for your neighbors." She paused. "You see, there's been a sort of smell coming from his apartment. I wouldn't say anything normally, but poor Betsy makes such a fuss every time we pass the door. Her nose is so sensitive. Isn't it, Betsy darling?"

My heart sank. It wasn't exactly the personal angle my father was looking for. I asked a few more questions, but it was pretty clear Dot didn't know Dr. Learner more than to say hello in the morning.

We had to listen to Dot talk about poor Betsy and her sensitive nose for another ten minutes before I managed to talk us out of there. Kevin was no help. He was enjoying his cookies too much.

"Well, that was a waste of time," I said after Dot shut the door. There were four more doors to go. I was starting to get a headache. "Come on," I said. "Let's see who's behind door number 207."

I raised my hand but didn't get the chance to knock.

"Not another step!" It might have been the gruff voice, or it might have been the very large hand on my shoulder, but I listened. I didn't move an inch.

(12

AFTER A SECOND that felt like a year, the hand let go of my shoulder. I saw Kevin breathe again, and I turned around and found myself face-to-face with the stomach of a very large man. I had to crane my neck to see his face. And even then, all I could see was the underside of his chin. He'd missed a spot shaving that morning.

"Are you the kids related to Dr. Learner?"

"Who are you?" I took a step back and got a better look at him. He was wearing a denim jumpsuit decorated with grease stains. It looked like he was the Drake Towers handyman. He had a large toolbox in his left hand and a roll of black plastic trash bags under his arm.

"I'm Mr. Ryder. I'm the apartment manager. Eunice called to tell me you two were poking around up here."

Eunice must have been the sparkling personality in 202.

Kevin got in front of me and gave Mr. Ryder a smile that could have made rocks melt. "We just want to find out where he's gone."

"You and me both." The man grunted. "The rent's due next week. But that isn't the problem."

"It isn't?" I asked.

"Well, not yet anyway. The real problem is the smell. The neighbors are starting to complain, and lord knows Eunice complains enough as it is already. But now that you two are here, I don't need to worry."

I had a feeling I knew where this was going, and I couldn't believe my luck.

Mr. Ryder got out his bunch of keys and started flicking through the keys until he found the one he wanted. He worked it off the ring and handed it to Kevin. He handed me the roll of trash bags.

"You're his relatives. You're responsible. Go clean it out."

"But we're kids," Kevin said before I could shut him up. This was a golden opportunity to search Dr. Learner's apartment, and he was about to blow it.

"Then call your parents and get them to come clean up this mess. I don't care. I want it gone."

"But—" Kevin started to say. I stomped on his foot, hard.

"We'll do our best," I said. "Are you coming with us?"

"Not a chance." Mr. Ryder grinned, and then he whistled

his way back down the walkway and up the steps to the third floor.

"Why did you tell him we'd clean the place?" Kevin looked at me like I was crazy.

"He gave us the key! We can search for clues."

"So we're not cleaning?"

"Of course not." I grabbed the key out of Kevin's hand and walked quickly down the walkway to 203.

Dot and Mr. Ryder were right. There was a bit of a smell sneaking out from around the edges of the door.

I put the key into the lock.

"Wait." Kevin stopped me. "You don't think *he's* in there, do you? You know, the smell?"

I paused and sniffed the air. "It smells like rotten food, not decomposition," I said. "Besides, I'm pretty sure Mr. Delgado said that they checked Dr. Learner's apartment. They wouldn't still be looking for him if he was in there."

"If you say so," said Kevin. His face was pale and slightly gray, like the underbelly of a fish.

"I do." I turned the key and opened the door.

The smell hit us like a fist. It was awful, a mix of musk and rot, old cheese and unwashed socks, and a million other things too disgusting to think about. Dr. Learner may have only been missing for two days, but whoever cleaned his apartment had been missing a lot longer.

107

"Get a window open," I said. My eyes watered with the smell of it all.

Kevin covered his nose and mouth with one hand and made his way across the room, struggling to unlock the catch on the window behind the couch. "This is so not worth twenty bucks," he said.

I pulled the neck of my T-shirt up over my nose and stepped inside. The apartment consisted of four rooms. The front door opened into the living room. To the right was the kitchen, and to the left the bedroom and bathroom. I stepped inside and let the door swing shut behind me.

"What are you doing? Keep it open. Let the smell out," Kevin said, uncovering his mouth and then immediately covering it again.

"Don't worry, we won't stay too long. I just want to have a quick look around." I wanted to see if that top-secret briefcase was there. It was a small chance, but possible. The mess in this place was a security system in itself.

Dr. Learner's apartment hadn't seen the business end of a mop in months. The living room was full of bookshelves, but they were empty, their contents pulled out and piled on the floor. Towers of books and binders, folders and files, grew out of the ground like a miniature city. I felt like Godzilla as I moved through the room. I snapped a few pictures with my phone, but I didn't think they were what Dad was after, at least not for the puff piece.

I checked the kitchen first, taking pictures as I went. Counters lined two walls and a small two-person table took up the third. At least, I guessed it was a table. I couldn't see the top of it.

There was a worrying crunch when I stepped onto the linoleum, like someone had spilled a box of cereal on the floor. I hoped it was cereal. I hoped harder than I'd ever hoped before, but the sound of buzzing and the swarm of flies around the sink were all clues that I shouldn't look down. I swallowed hard and told the pretzel I'd eaten earlier to stay in my stomach where it belonged.

I rooted through the cabinets quickly, touching as little as possible. No briefcase. The freezer was empty except for a half-full can of coffee beans and an empty ice tray. The refrigerator was covered with magnets and reminder notes. Some of them were normal, like a list for bread, cheese, and milk. But there were also notes filled with complex equations and formulas. I saw a few that I recognized, but most of them were too advanced. I took a few more pictures, just in case Dr. Learner had posted the formula for invisibility on his refrigerator before he left town.

Underneath the top layer of notes, I found a child's

drawing, the edges of the paper slightly brittle with age. It was a portrait of Dr. Learner, with a giant head and tiny legs and a smile that was bigger than his face. He was wearing a wizard hat and holding a wand. I wondered who drew it. Dr. Learner didn't have any kids, or nieces and nephews. At least that's what it said in the Delgado file. Whoever drew it thought Dr. Learner was a pretty great guy. I opened the refrigerator and shut it again. Fast. You could tell me there was a diamond the size of a tennis ball in there and I still wouldn't open it again.

Gagging, I stumbled back into the living room. Kevin had his head out of the window. Some help he was.

Most of the clutter was in the middle of the living room, radiating out from the couch. So I moved along the edges, making my way to the bedroom. A large oil painting of a peaceful mountain scene hung in the middle of the wall surrounded by pictures of family and friends. One photo in particular caught my eye. Dr. Learner stood with one arm around Sammy's shoulder, the two of them smiling like idiots and holding up a small silver trophy. Squinting, I could just make out the words *Second Place* and *Science Fair*. I suddenly had a pretty good idea who the artist was of that picture in the kitchen. I also knew why Sammy was so insistent on helping me solve this case. He wanted his hero back.

My stomach turned in a way that had nothing to do with the smell. I wondered what I'd say to Sammy if I couldn't find

Dr. Learner. I pushed the thought away quickly. There was no point in worrying about that now. If I wanted to find Dr. Learner, all I could do was keep looking.

The bedroom was a bit better than the rest of the apartment. The closet doors stood open, its contents, hangers and all, heaped across the bed. By the looks of things, Dr. Learner hadn't eaten any food in here, just drunk cups and cups and cups of coffee. Every surface that wasn't covered with books or clothes had a paper coffee cup on it. Not all of them were empty.

As I looked around, I couldn't shake the feeling that Kevin and I weren't the first ones to search the place. Besides the mess, things were just slightly askew, as if they'd been moved and put back, but not in quite the right place. But I didn't think it was the police. They wouldn't have been so careful. I didn't see a briefcase anywhere. Even when I gathered the courage to look under the bed.

I stuck my head in the bathroom. It was surprisingly clean. Actually, it was so clean I wondered if it was ever used. I opened the medicine cabinet. The top shelf had a toothbrush and toothpaste and five boxes of dental floss. The middle shelf was for all the soaps and shaving things. But the bottom shelf was empty. I looked closer. There were several water stains, small circular ones. The size of a prescription medicine bottle.

"It looks like someone came and got his medicine," I said as I stepped back into the bedroom. That meant either Dr. Learner had been planning to escape, or whoever took him had come back to get the bottles.

I stopped. There was an odd rectangle of clean space between the bed and the wall. It was partially hidden behind a large tower of textbooks, so I hadn't seen it from the other side of the room. No coffee cups, no books, no dust even. Something used to sit there, and it had been moved. Something the size and shape of a briefcase.

"Numbers, hey." Kevin hurried into the bedroom, his voice croaky.

"Yes, yes, we can go in a minute." I took a picture of the empty space.

"No, that's not it. Someone's coming."

"What?" I asked.

"I saw some guy out of the window."

I didn't understand why Kevin sounded so frantic.

"So?" I said. "It's not like we're not supposed to be here. We've got permission."

"Yeah, but I don't think he does," Kevin said.

The sound of breaking glass cleared up any other questions I might have had.

Someone was breaking in.

(13

"HIDE!" I HISSED.

Kevin made a move to get under the bed. I dragged him back. Not even Kevin Jordan deserved what was under there. Besides, we might need to leave in a hurry, and it was easier to make a run for it if you weren't flat on your stomach.

"Get behind the door."

Kevin jumped over a pile of laundry and squeezed behind me into the space between the bedroom door and the wall. I could feel Kevin's breath on the back of my neck, and the stray hairs that escaped from my braid tickled like torture.

If I pressed my eye against the crack between the door and the frame, I had a clear view of Dr. Learner's front door. The window next to it was broken, a slight breeze wafting the curtains into the room. I watched as a hand reached through them and groped for the door handle. Then the fingers closed around it

113

and Dr. Learner's door swung open. It looked like whoever had searched Dr. Learner's apartment before was back to finish the job. But if they were back, did that mean the briefcase was still missing? And if so, where was it?

"Oh, man, what do we do? What do we do?" Kevin said. His fingers dug into my shoulders.

"Shhh," I said. "It's fine. Just keep quiet." I couldn't think with Kevin panicking in my ear.

The burglar came into Dr. Learner's apartment. He had a Philadelphia Flyers cap pulled down low over his eyes. The rest of his face was hidden by his enormous hand as he tried to block out the smell. But I'd seen that gigantic upside-down trapezoid before. In fact, I'd seen it that very morning.

Kevin's fingers dug in deeper. Tomorrow I'd have ten finger-sized bruises.

"He's going into the kitchen. Quick," I said. We moved from behind the door and into the living room.

"What are you doing?" Kevin asked in a low voice, as I took an office chair from under a pile of pizza boxes and carried it gently to the front door, blocking the only escape route. I took out my phone and waited.

"Trust me," I said, sitting down. I could hear gagging coming from the kitchen, and then the burglar came back into the living room, bent over and holding his stomach.

"Hello, Graham. Say cheese."

The tiny light from my phone flashed. Graham Davidson stood frozen in the middle of the room, half standing, half squatting. He looked like a cat clinging to a curtain. He stared at me and then at the door behind me and then at me again. It was like he was stuck in some sort of fight-or-flight loop.

"Wait, you know him?" Kevin asked.

"He's Dr. Learner's lab assistant. We met this morning." I looked at the time on my phone and then back at Graham. "You must have left work early."

Graham opened his mouth, but he didn't make a sound. I couldn't even tell if he was breathing. I guess I would have been shocked too if I'd broken into my boss's place and been caught in the act by two kids. It was either that or he'd left the fridge open for too long and the smell had broken his brain.

I tried some gentle prodding. "The briefcase isn't here, if that's what you're after. I checked."

That did the trick. Graham let out his breath in a long sigh and came back to life. He looked up at the ceiling like he was asking someone *Why does this stuff always happen to me?* Then he flopped down onto the couch. A cloud of dust mushroomed around him.

"That's that, then." He coughed. "When you came asking questions at the office, I thought there might be a chance it was all still here. I should have known it was too good to be true."

I could feel Kevin relaxing. I shot him a look that said, *Let me do the talking*. It didn't look like Graham had been here before, so he probably wasn't the one who turned over the place. But I still wanted to ask him some questions, and I didn't want Kevin giving the game away.

"What was too good to be true?"

"Like I'd tell you. Sorry, kid. Go fish."

I held up my phone. "Too bad," I said. "I guess I'll have to send Mr. Delgado that photo and tell him all about your little visit to Dr. Learner's apartment. He's pretty smart. I'm sure he'll figure out what you were up to. I wonder what happens to a lab assistant who tries to steal company secrets? I'm sure there are plenty of other PhDs who'd love a job with Delgado Industries."

Graham stared at me and leaned forward in his seat. I could see his fingers twitch. He licked his lips like he was getting ready for something. Behind me I could feel Kevin getting ready to make a move of his own. I held up my hand to stop them both.

"Don't even think about it," I said. "I've got my finger on the send button. I'll press it before you can stand up."

"Stop," Graham said. He held up his hands. "Stop. I'll talk. But you gotta promise not to tell Delgado. He'll fire me in a second. I'll never get a job in a lab again."

"Fine." I lowered the phone but kept my finger on the

button. I didn't want Graham making any sudden moves in my direction. "So, what are you doing here?"

"It isn't what you think," Graham started, then he stopped, searching for the right words.

"I'm listening."

"OK, maybe it *is* what you think. But why not? I figure Dr. Learner's already run off with his research. So why shouldn't I look for his notes? I worked on that project too, technically. I should get some of the credit." Graham bent forward again, bracing his elbows on his knees.

"Go on."

He glared at me, but he kept talking.

"After Dr. Learner went missing, I got a call from Chronos. They asked if I'd worked on the project. If I thought I could reproduce Dr. Learner's results. They offered to hire me. And not just as an assistant. They offered to give me a job as a lead researcher."

It looked like Dr. Learner wasn't the only one Chronos was trying to steal from Delgado Industries.

"So you took the job?"

"Not exactly." Graham's large fingers picked at a patch of dirt on his knee.

"Oh, I get it. You couldn't reproduce the results."

"As I said, Dr. Learner got really secretive about six months ago. He wouldn't let me into his office. And he stopped

117

having me type up his notes. That's when he must have made that breakthrough you were talking about. He must have known how much people would pay for . . ." Graham paused and looked at me, his eyes narrowed.

"For the technology to make an invisibility suit?" I finished the sentence for him.

Graham gasped, then he choked. "How did you know about the suit?" he managed between coughs.

"That doesn't matter," I said. I thought about getting Graham a drink of water, but I wasn't sure there was a clean glass in the place, so I waited until he finished coughing before I asked any more questions. It took a while.

"So you think he's made a breakthrough that will make it possible to create an invisibility suit?" I asked once I was sure Graham wasn't going to choke.

"I don't think he's just come up with the theory of the technology. I think he did it! He built the suit!"

"But that's crazy," I said, wishing I felt as sure as I sounded. It was one thing to tell Della and Dad that making an invisibility suit was impossible. But if a scientist like Graham Davidson thought it was true, maybe I was wrong.

"I thought so too," said Graham. "But don't you see? It's the only way he could have disappeared the way he did. He waited overnight in the office, and when I came in that morning he put on the suit to become invisible. When I opened the door to see if he was there, he just walked out. He could be here watching us right now and we'd never know."

I shivered, just for a moment, imagining a world where invisible people watched you from the corners of your room. And then I shook it off. No, even if Graham Davidson thought it was possible, I still couldn't believe it. Not without real, solid proof.

"Wait. What are you two talking about?" Kevin couldn't keep quiet any longer. The words almost exploded out of him.

Graham looked at Kevin and then at me. "Who is this kid?"

"He's . . ." I tried to think of a word that would be reassuring but also honest. I came up blank. "He's helping me out on the case."

Kevin said nothing. The idea of helping me must have shocked him into silence.

"Well, I'm not saying another word. Now delete that photo and let me get out of this cesspit."

"Wait. Just one more question. What do you think an invisibility suit would look like? How big would it be?" I tilted my head to the side. "Do you think it could fit inside a briefcase?"

Graham Davidson stood up and loomed over us. Any advantage I'd had before was overshadowed, literally.

"I said no more questions."

"Fine." I made a show of deleting the picture. He didn't need to answer. I could tell I was right. Graham wasn't looking for

Dr. Learner's notes in that briefcase. He was looking for the finished suit.

We helped Graham Davidson cover the window he'd broken with a piece of cardboard from an old pizza box and some duct tape, and then we left. The air on the other side of the door smelled as sweet as a fresh box of No. 2 pencils. I gulped it in. I needed a shower. Not just any shower. I needed the kind of shower people got after a radiation leak.

Graham pushed past us and took the stairs two at a time. He was in his car and driving out of the parking lot before Kevin and I reached the second floor landing.

At the bottom of the steps, there was a door labeled MANAGEMENT. I looked around quickly to make sure Mr. Ryder wasn't going to grab us and make us finish the cleanup we were supposed to have started.

"Ugh, I feel disgusting." Kevin shuddered.

I put my ear to the door. All quiet. Mr. Ryder must have been busy somewhere else in the building.

"Come on," I said, dropping Dr. Learner's key into the mailbox mounted on the wall next to the door. "Let's get out of here."

"So, is all that invisibility stuff for real?" Kevin asked as we walked across the crumbling asphalt to where we'd left our bikes.

"I don't know. Davidson seems to think so, and he has a PhD. He told me so himself."

"Yeah, but is that Learner guy really that smart? I mean, look at his place. Who lives like that?"

I hated to admit it, but Kevin Jordan had a point. Dr. Learner's apartment had me asking myself a lot of questions about the so-called genius. It also had me asking myself when was the last time I cleaned my room.

The trip hadn't been a total disaster, though. I may not have sniffed out much of a personal angle for my father, but I got Graham to confirm our suspicions.

Dr. Learner was working on an invisibility suit, or at least the first stages of one.

And Chronos was trying to get their hands on it.

But I couldn't believe Dr. Learner would sell it to them of his own free will. Not after seeing that drawing on his refrigerator. Or maybe I just didn't want to believe it. I didn't want to have to tell Sammy his hero had betrayed him.

I crouched down to unlock the bike chain. While I was down there, I made a note to throw away my shoes. Kevin stood next to me, leaning back on the chain-link fence. The metal scraped and rattled as it moved.

"Hey," Kevin said. "What would you do if you could turn invisible?"

I didn't look up. "I don't know. Avoid having this conversation?"

"That's so boring."

The lock popped and I stood up, passing Kevin his bike.

"I know what I'd do." He grinned.

I didn't ask. I was pretty sure I'd be happier not knowing. I just wound up the lock chain and started pushing my bike toward the exit. Kevin pushed his bike beside me.

"I have to admit, it was pretty cool when you took the photo of that guy. Like BAM, we've got you now, sucker! I thought he was going to cry. I can't believe you deleted it, though."

"What makes you think I deleted it?"

"Uh, I saw you?"

I raised an eyebrow. "I sent myself a copy first. I'm not stupid."

I actually kind of enjoyed the look of admiration on Kevin's face. I was just about to smile when something silver caught my eye.

"What?" Kevin asked.

"It's nothing," I said. "At least, I think it's nothing."

I peered casually through the chain-link fence at the cars parked across the road. If it was the same car, I didn't want them to know I'd caught on. "It's just I thought there was a car following me and my dad this morning. I've been a bit jumpy since then."

"What kind of car?" Kevin was looking across the street too.

"A silver Mercedes."

"Like that one?" Kevin asked. He pointed his finger through the fence. Almost immediately, the silver car started up and pulled away, kicking up loose gravel and stones onto the car parked behind it.

"Yeah," I said. "Exactly like that one."

(14

KEVIN'S MOUTH HUNG open as the Mercedes drove away.

"Wait, were they following you?"

I checked the license plate against the photo I took that morning. They matched. "Looks like it."

"But why?"

It was a good question, but I could take a guess at the answer.

It was someone from Chronos.

I already knew they wanted the research, and they were willing to use Graham Davidson to steal it. It didn't seem that odd that they'd follow the person Mr. Delgado hired to find Dr. Learner too. Maybe Dr. Learner had to disappear to hide from them. Maybe they'd already kidnapped him. If they were willing to do that much for just the research, imagine what they'd do for the actual suit. I shuddered: Dr. Learner might be in serious trouble.

"So, what are you going to do? Call the police?"

"Do you think the police would believe me?" I pushed my bike out onto the pavement, and Kevin followed. "I'll tell Mr. Delgado about it, and my dad. It's annoying, but I don't think it's dangerous. It's not like they'll do anything to me until I lead them to Dr. Learner's invisibility suit. And the chances that I'll find it are really low anyway."

Kevin opened his mouth to answer back, but he never got the chance. He was interrupted by a plain white van. It stopped right in front of us, and the door slid open. The first thing I thought when I saw the inside was, *Oh, no, not again.*

"Alice Jones?" An official-looking man wearing official-looking clothes leaned out of the van. Even his haircut looked official. "Would you mind stepping into the van for a moment? Agent Reed would like to speak with you."

Right. Like I was just going to climb into an unmarked van. Kevin must have been thinking the same thing. He had a death grip on the hem of my shirt, ready to stop me if I made a move.

"Can I see some ID?" Behind him I could see speakers and screens and displays with impressive flashing lights mounted on the inner wall. There was also a small coffeepot in the far corner, which was probably more important than all of the other high-tech gear combined.

The man handed me a black wallet. I flipped it open and saw a bronze badge and a photo ID printed with the letters *FBI*. I looked at the badge, then at the man. It looked real. Besides, no one would use the name Ian Gerber on a fake ID.

I climbed into the van, dragging Kevin along with me. I hoped whatever they wanted wouldn't take too long. I didn't think Della would believe that dinner was late because the FBI wanted a chat.

Agent Gerber pointed us toward a woman in the back of the van before he shut the door. Then he sat down in the corner and got out a newspaper. I noticed he'd filled in the Sudoku in pen. I also noticed he'd gotten the top right corner wrong, but didn't think now was the time to mention it.

The woman handed me her ID badge and smiled a nice, warm, motherly smile that made me want to confide in her. I bet the FBI trained her how to do that. She wore a boxy blue suit, wrinkled like it had been slept in.

"All right, Agent Reed," I said as I handed back the badge. "What do you want?"

"It's nothing for you to worry about. We just have a few questions about Dr. Learner and his research."

"You mean the invis—"

I put my hand over Kevin's mouth before he could blurt it out.

"Oh, don't worry. We already know about Dr. Learner's

new project. We have our own sources. We're interested in signing a contract, but there are other parties interested too. We need to know how far he's gotten with the technology, and if he's given it to anyone else. It's very important you tell us everything you know. This could be a matter of national security."

Great, I thought, *now I'll have to tell Sammy his friend might be a traitor as well as a thief.*

"And you think I can help you?"

"Mr. Delgado did give you special access to Delgado Industries. The Bureau thought it was a little unusual, but sometimes an outside eye can see things that people too close to a project can't. Or maybe Mr. Delgado had another reason for hiring you?" Agent Reed watched me very closely. It felt like she was accusing me of something. I just didn't know what.

"Why else would he hire her?" Kevin said. "Everyone at school knows Alice is great at solving mysteries."

He must have been angry. His face was bright red. I was too shocked to speak. Kevin Jordan had just stood up for me.

Agent Reed smiled again, a little bit cooler this time.

"We aren't asking her to solve this for us," she said. "We're just asking her to tell us what she knows. And we're asking very nicely"—she turned to me—"for now."

I paused. I wasn't sure how much Mr. Delgado wanted the government to know. I mean, if he was trying to land a big contract, did he really want me sharing? Then again, it's not like

I was actually working for Mr. Delgado. As far as I was concerned, he'd offered me the ten-thousand-dollar reward for finding Dr. Learner just like he'd offered it to anyone who read any newspaper in the area. And so far, all I'd gotten for my pains was a lot of trouble with a capital T. The sooner someone found Dr. Learner, the better. I didn't care if it was me or the feds.

"What do you want to know?"

"Everything."

So I told Agent Reed what I knew. And as I told her, I realized that what I knew didn't even amount to a hill of beans.

Dr. Learner had disappeared. Chronos wanted his research, but they hadn't gotten it yet, so they tried to use Graham Davidson to get it for them. Only Graham hadn't found anything either. It made me wonder if there was any research to find. I felt like a dog chasing its tail. I was pretty sure Chronos was behind Dr. Learner's disappearance. They seemed like they'd do anything to get their hands on that invisibility suit.

I stopped talking for a moment, and thought about what I'd just said.

If Chronos was asking Graham Davidson to reproduce Dr. Learner's work, it meant that they didn't already have it. They were probably following me hoping that I would lead them to Dr. Learner or to his briefcase. I'd felt pretty smug about my deduction before. But now I realized it meant my main suspect had to be innocent. Chronos R & D wouldn't be trying to find Dr. Learner if they'd kidnapped him.

"Wait," Agent Reed said, stopping me mid-sentence. "You say Dr. Learner's lab assistant thinks there's a functioning prototype?" Agent Reed bore down on me, her motherly brown eyes suddenly turning professional.

Kevin couldn't stop himself. "Yeah, he thinks that Dr. Learner used the invisibility suit to escape!"

"That's what Graham says, but it doesn't seem possible," I chimed in.

Agent Reed wasn't listening to me anymore. She'd clearly gotten what she was after. She turned her back on us and picked up her phone, waving at the other agent to show us out. He did, quickly.

As we climbed out of the van and back onto the street, I could hear Agent Reed saying, "Hello, Director. We've confirmed it."

But I didn't hear anything after that. The door slammed shut before she could say another word.

Kevin turned to me. "Why didn't you tell them about the car that's been following you?"

"Agent Reed didn't seem interested in *me*." Plus, I didn't like her or Agent Gerber, and the thought of asking them for help made my teeth ache. But Kevin had a point. I might not get another chance to report them.

"Hey!" I banged my palm against the side of the van.

The door slid open again. Agent Gerber looked down at me. He clearly hadn't been to the "friendly faces for children" class yet.

"What?"

"There's one more thing." I got out my phone and started scrolling through the pictures. "A car's been following me since Mr. Delgado asked me to look for Dr. Learner."

"Really?" he said. I could tell he didn't believe me.

"Yes, really. I have the license plate number. It followed me and my dad home from Delgado Industries, and it was here just now. They drove away in a hurry the second this genius"—I jerked my head in Kevin's direction—"pointed at them."

I handed Agent Gerber my phone. Agent Gerber looked at the picture and clicked his teeth. "Fine, I'll make a note of the license plate in the file. Be careful walking home."

He shut the door again. I got the feeling he wouldn't open it again no matter how hard I pounded on it.

"Wow," said Kevin. "That was the FBI. We talked to the FBI."

For someone who lived to break the rules, Kevin seemed pretty excited.

"Hey, wait a minute," he said. "If they were watching Dr. Learner's apartment, why didn't they come and help us? They knew we were in there, and they must have seen that Davidson guy breaking in. We could have been in danger!"

"The same reason the guys in the silver Mercedes didn't come rushing in. They wanted to see what we'd find."

"Are you going to keep looking for him? For the doctor?"

"I don't know. Maybe." It was a lie. I knew I'd keep looking. I was as bad as my father once I got started on a problem. Leaving it unsolved would drive me crazy. I didn't even care about proving Mr. Delgado wrong anymore, or at least not much. I just wanted to be able to tell Sammy the truth. Even if I didn't like the way he followed me around all the time, he deserved to know what had really happened to his friend.

Kevin stared at me.

"What?"

"You're not normal, are you?" he said after a long pause. "Here, give me your phone."

He took it out of my hand and started pressing buttons.

"There, that's my number. Call me if you think you're going to find him. Don't go alone."

"You're joking."

Kevin handed back the phone. "You've seen movies, right? All I'm saying is, don't be that person. Call me or your dad. Whatever."

"Fine, I get it. I'll call someone. Now can we go? I told my sister I'd cook dinner." I threw my leg over my bike and pushed off. Kevin was right behind me.

"You have a sister?"

I don't know how it happened. But somehow I found myself talking to Kevin Jordan. No, not talking. I was telling him things. I told him about Della, and how the audition process was making her a little crazy. How Dad was busy on a story and now Mom probably thought he was neglecting us. I told him how I wished I could solve my family like they were some sort of math problem, balance the equation and get a nice neat answer.

"That way, maybe I could make everyone equally happy, you know? And it would be fair."

I regretted it the instant the words were out of my mouth. But there was nothing I could do to take them back, and trying to cover them up would make it even worse.

"Anyway, enough about me," I said. "Isn't this your street?"

"Nah, I'm going into the city. I'll ride with you."

Side by side in the late-afternoon haze, it was hard to tell if he was teasing me or trying to be nice.

It was a relief when we finally got to my house. I pushed my bike up the steps as quickly as I could. Kevin offered to help, but I told him he'd done enough for one day.

"Listen, about the money . . ." Kevin put his foot on the bottom step, but I stopped him.

"My dad isn't home, so you'll have to come by some other time."

"No, it's fine. Just tell him to forget about it."

Kevin hopped off the step and back onto his bike.

"What do you mean?" I called after him.

"I don't need the money," he yelled back, and then he rode away, pedaling like his life depended on it.

The list of things that made no sense just kept getting bigger.

(15

THE INSIDE OF our house was quiet. Dad probably had to stay at the paper until his deadline. I ran upstairs to take a shower and get some fresh clothes. There was no way I was touching food until I was clean. As I opened my bedroom door, I took a deep breath and prepared myself to pretend I hadn't heard a word of Della and Mom's conversation. Just because I don't like acting doesn't mean I'm no good at it.

Della preparing for an audition was a force of nature. Specifically, a tornado. My room looked like it had been turned upside down and shaken. Hard. Clothes from all of the drawers and closet lay scattered across the floor and draped over the furniture. Sheet music and manuscript pages littered the bed. The air bed was propped up, covering the window. Della was doing a split in the middle of the floor, her head pressed all the way down to her knee. I picked my way across the room and found a clean pair of pajamas.

"Oh my God, Alice. You stink." Della sat up, turned her waist 180 degrees, and put her nose to her other knee. "What have you been doing?"

"I don't want to talk about it. I'm going to shower."

"Mom wanted to say hello. You should call her back."

I waved my hand but didn't respond. Phone calls with Mom lasted hours, not minutes, and I didn't have that kind of time to spare. I also wasn't sure I wanted to talk to Mom right now, not after what I'd overheard Della saying. My stomach twisted guiltily, and I promised it I'd call as soon as the case was over.

I started to walk out, stepped on something sharp, and hopped the rest of the way to the bathroom. I turned on the shower and stood under the spray with my eyes closed. The hot water stung where my scalp was sunburned, but it was worth it. I used the rough side of the sponge to scrub myself clean. I wished I could scrub the day away as easily as the dirt. It had been nothing but one long string of disappointment and dead ends.

Everyone I'd talked to seemed to think that Dr. Learner was out there, turning invisible. I just didn't buy it. Sure, one day someone would figure out how to bend enough light to make an invisibility suit, but Dr. Learner made his breakthrough six months ago. Even if he'd developed new technology that would make an invisibility suit possible, there was no way six months was enough time to build a working prototype. Especially if he didn't let anyone help him. Something else had to be going on. The problem was, all anyone had seen was the tape of Dr. Learner disappearing from a locked room, and they jumped to conclusions before learning all the facts. It was sloppy, bad logic, and it made my skin itch.

I tipped my head back to rinse the bubbles out of my hair and found myself wondering what the point was. If Dr. Learner had finished the suit, why did he use it to disappear at all? And what was he using it for now? I knew he hadn't sold it to Chronos, since they were still out there looking for it. Besides, if he needed money, he could have just taken the diamonds. I breathed out hard, blowing water off my lips.

No matter how I did the math, Dr. Learner running away by himself didn't add up. Someone else must have made him disappear. But if that was true, why didn't we see them on the security tape? I shampooed my hair again. If I wanted to find Dr. Learner, I needed to figure out how he got out of his office. I must have missed something when we were there. Once I knew how he did it, I'd know who helped him. And if I knew that, finding him would be simpler than solving $x = 1 + 1$.

My phone rang, and I climbed out of the shower, dripping water all over the floor.

"Hey, Dad."

"Alice, I've been trying to call you. I need to put this story to bed. Make my day and tell me you found some nice, juicy personal details for me?" I could hear him typing furiously on the other end of the line. Dad must be the only person who can carry on a conversation about one thing while writing about something entirely different. It was like he had two brains. Maybe that was why he couldn't sit still for more than two seconds at a time.

"Sorry, Dad. I got nothing."

"What do you mean 'nothing'?"

"Dr. Learner's apartment was a health hazard. The smell almost killed me. If there was a cat anywhere, it was dead."

"Ouch."

Dad paused. Even the typing stopped. I felt rotten.

"Listen, Sammy told me Dr. Learner and Mr. Delgado really were good friends when they were at the University of Pennsylvania together. Mr. Delgado brought Dr. Learner back from California so they could work together. Also, Sammy really looked up to him, like a mentor or something. They did science projects together. That's an angle, isn't it?"

"Hmmm." The typing started again. "Best friends build a business together. Dr. Learner is kind to children; yeah, there's something there. OK, I'll be home late tonight. Take care of dinner, all right?"

"I'm just going to do it now."

I put my hair up and climbed into my clean clothes. I left the ones I'd been wearing at Dr. Learner's in the middle of the bathroom floor. I'd come back later with some rubber gloves to deal with those.

Downstairs I got a box of macaroni and cheese out of the cupboard and put a pan of water on the stove to boil. It wasn't gourmet dining, but it was full of carbs. Just what the diva ordered.

I was chopping up hot dogs to throw into the sauce when the phone rang again. This time it was the house phone, not my cell phone.

"Alice? It's me, Sammy. I wanted to talk to you about the case. I heard you went to Dr. Learner's apartment. Uh, I was wondering if you . . . uh . . . Did you find anything?" Sammy asked, doing a bad job trying to sound casual.

"I'm kind of busy right now, Sammy. This isn't a good time." I wasn't lying either. The pan had boiled over and the stove was spitting and hissing.

"Oh," Sammy said. I could feel his dejection through the phone line, like he was sending it down the wire. I should have just hung up, but I didn't. Seeing the state of Dr. Learner's apartment had made me realize that being a loner could lead to scary situations. Or maybe I'd inhaled something poisonous. Mostly, though, now that I knew how much Sammy admired Dr. Learner, I felt sorry for him.

"Look, Sammy, I can't talk now. But I want to go back to the lab tomorrow . . ."

"Great, we can go together. It'll be great! What time do you want me to pick you up?"

"No, I'll . . ." I was going to tell him I'd meet him there. But then I remembered that Dad's story would keep him really busy, so I might not have a lift. And I was pretty sure Sammy had a car and chauffeur allocated for his personal use, and not just for lifts to and from school. "Fine, pick me up at nine. I'll see you tomorrow."

I hung up the phone, cutting off Sammy's excited babble, and drained the pasta before it turned to mush. It wasn't until I'd set the table that I realized how odd Sammy's call really was. How had he known I'd been to Dr. Learner's apartment? And what did he think I might have found? He'd acted strange when he came over earlier too. The way he fidgeted on the couch. That kid was hiding something. And tomorrow I was going to find out what.

Della and I ate dinner in character. She was Annie. I was Miss Hannigan. It was a flashback to my entire childhood. I put on my best evil voice and told Della she was a "rotten orphan."

Della laughed. "You know what this reminds me of? Back when we were on the pageant circuit together and Mom used to make us practice our act at the dinner table."

"Don't remind me." Mom had entered us in the Little Miss Friendship pageant when we were four. Della won and I took runner-up. I had the teeny-weeny trophy at the back of my bedroom closet to prove it.

After that, Della got the performance bug. She got it bad. And my mom loved it. The problem was, I didn't. And no one believed me. It took me three pageants to figure out how to get out of it.

I mooned the audience.

I still laugh when I remember the look on that head judge's face.

"I'll never understand how you gave it up," Della said. "Don't you want to get back out there?" Her eyes were full of pity. Like I was missing out on something.

"Nope." I speared a piece of hot dog and put it in my mouth. End of discussion.

Della took a dainty bite and chewed thoughtfully.

"I called Mom, like you said. She was sad she didn't get to talk to you."

I swallowed too soon, and the piece of hot dog went down my throat in a lump. "I had to go out."

"She says Italy is amazing. She said if we want she'll get us tickets and we can spend a week with her at the end of the summer."

"What about *Annie*?"

"Even if I get the part, I'd be sharing it with two other girls. I'm sure I'd be able to get one week off. Even actresses get vacations, you know. What do you think? Wouldn't it be amazing?"

"I guess," I said slowly. It wasn't that I didn't want to go to Italy. It was just that I knew what a trip to Italy with Della and my mom meant. It meant a week of shopping and shows and not a lot else.

If Dad came too, then there'd be someone to come with me to do my kind of things. But you can't exactly ask someone to invite her ex-husband to the party.

"Well, you should talk to her," Della said. "I think it would be fun."

"Of course it'll be fun for *you*. You and Mom like doing all of the same things."

"What are you talking about?"

"If we go to Italy, I'll want to see things like the Archimedes museum or go on a tour of Renaissance architecture."

Della groaned and rolled her eyes.

"See?" I pointed. "See! That face. That face is exactly how I'll feel when you two drag me to see another show or go to another dress fitting."

"But Alice, those things are normal. Everyone likes shows and shopping."

"Just forget it." It was the story of my life. Everyone understood that Della loved being onstage and that she hated math.

Because that was normal. But when I said I loved math and hated performing, people looked at me like I had a screw loose. And because the things I liked weren't normal, I didn't have any right to ask other people to do them with me.

"Fine, but you need to talk to Mom." Della held up her hands. "I'm not doing it for you. Come on, let's run the scene one more time."

"No." Maybe it was childish, but I didn't want to play "acting" anymore. "I already ran the lines with you eleven times. You know them by heart. *I* know them by heart. Give it a rest. Besides, I have work to do."

"That case? Are you serious?" Della looked at me like I'd just refused to give her a blood transfusion.

"Yes. I'm serious."

"That guy only hired you so you'd hang out with his kid. Why are you wasting your time on some stupid mystery you're never going to solve?"

"Why are *you* wasting your time auditioning for a part you're never going to get?" I shot back. It was a low blow and I knew it, but it was out before I could stop myself.

Della stood up from the counter. Her lips pursed; her eyes narrowed. She told me that we were no longer on speaking terms without saying a single word. Then she turned on her heel and walked away, her blonde hair bouncing angrily as she climbed the stairs. The hair was a nice touch. It said, *I'll show you.*

Della was going to get that part just to prove me wrong. Well, two could play at that game.

I got out the Delgado file and spread the pages out on the floor in front of the couch. If she could get a part out of spite, then I could solve a case that way. There had to be something in all of those papers, some clue to how Dr. Learner had escaped. I looked at the pictures. I read the eyewitness statements. But the more I looked, the less I saw. It was like Delgado had put together a file with no real clues on purpose.

Kevin Jordan's question popped into my head. What would I do if I could turn invisible? I didn't really know. It wasn't like there was anyone I wanted to spy on. I could use it to hide from Sammy, or Della when she was being a diva, but it's not like hiding would solve my problems. It might be fun to sneak into the university and go to some advanced math classes. (They won't even consider me until I turn sixteen.) But that was just a fantasy. There couldn't really be an invisibility suit, could there?

I leaned back on the couch and held the floor plan of the Delgado Industries office building over my head. Maybe the light would shine through it and reveal a secret message. It was as good as any of the other ideas I'd had. And with everyone else running around talking about invisibility suits, it didn't seem all that farfetched.

*

143

When I opened my eyes, the room was dark. Someone had taken the Delgado Industries floor plan out of my hands and covered me with a blanket. Dad. I could hear him typing from the other side of his office door. He must still be working on the story. The real story, that is, not the puff piece his editor wanted. I'd have to tell him all about the rest of my day in the morning. He'd be over the moon when I told him the FBI was involved.

I thought about going upstairs and sneaking into my room, but it seemed like too much trouble. Della was in my bed, and the air mattress would still be propped up against the window. So I just stretched out where I was and fell asleep listening to the comforting clatter of Dad's keyboard.

(16

I WOKE UP at seven with bird's-nest hair and dents on the side of my face from using the corduroy couch cushion as a pillow. I had a crick in my neck that felt like an ice pick.

Dad was rushing around the kitchen, trying to eat his breakfast and get ready for work at the same time. He had a square of toast in his mouth and a cup of coffee in his hand. Every move was a disaster waiting to happen. Della stood still, eating a bowl of porridge with one leg stretched up on the counter like it was a ballet barre.

"Morning, sweetie," Dad said. "I'll be late again today, but call me if you need anything. Either of you."

Dad gulped down the dregs of his coffee and put his water bottle in his bag before giving me a kiss on the forehead. His chin was rough with two days' worth of stubble. Then he kissed Della and ran out the door.

As the door banged shut, I realized I hadn't told him about my meeting with the FBI or the silver Mercedes that had been following me. But he was already gone. I'd have to tell him later. Until then, I'd just have to be careful. I shambled into the kitchen and poured myself the last of the coffee from the pot. Della moved out of my way, but didn't say a word. She still wasn't talking to me. We finished our breakfast in silence.

Sammy showed up right on time. He arrived in a black town car, probably the same car that had "picked me up" from school two days ago. It seemed like a lot longer ago than that. I'd spent the past two days chasing my tail, and I was exhausted. I gathered up the papers from the Delgado file and stuffed them into my messenger bag. I could feel Della's eyes on me every time I turned my back. I guess the town car was pretty impressive. But I wasn't in the mood to explain. I slung my bag over my shoulder and walked out of the door without looking back.

I scanned the street carefully as I walked down our front steps. No silver cars in sight. I didn't waste any time climbing through the door that Sammy's driver held open for me. It felt good to be behind tinted windows.

I let Sammy talk about the case for the first couple of minutes, while I kept busy checking the windows to make sure we weren't being followed. He spoke at a terrifying pace, words forming and tumbling out on top of each other like cars on the highway heading for a crash. After we'd gone through three intersections with no sign of the silver Mercedes, I started to relax. I didn't know where they were, but they weren't after me, and that was good enough.

Sammy was still talking a mile a minute. I hoped he stayed talkative. I had some questions and I wanted answers.

"Sammy." I interrupted him in the middle of a story about the time he and Dr. Learner built a hovercraft. He stopped jabbering and tilted his head eagerly to one side. "How did you know I went to Dr. Learner's apartment yesterday?" I asked as casually as I could. It wasn't like I was accusing him of anything, but it did seem strange. He'd already had his dad kidnap me over to play. For all I knew, Mr. Delgado was having me followed. Maybe I'd been wrong about the silver Mercedes. Maybe it wasn't Chronos's car, maybe it was Mr. Delgado's.

"Oh, I called your house. No one was home, so I phoned your dad. I would have called you, but I don't have your cell number."

He looked at me hopefully, but I didn't bite. The last thing I needed were phone calls from Sammy. But it answered the question. I guess I was lucky he hadn't decided to come over and help.

"OK, that makes sense," I said. Dad exchanged numbers with everyone he met, just in case they ever turned into a source. I shook my shoulders, trying to lose the feeling that someone was watching my every move. The case was making me jumpy, and it was getting hard to think straight.

"I'm sorry I couldn't come over and help you. It would have been great! I even got all this detective stuff." He pulled his backpack onto the seat between us and unzipped it so I could see inside. He had a notebook, a magnifying glass, a small fingerprint brush and vial of printing powder, and a listening device that looked like an MP3 player. Actually, the listening device looked pretty cool, but the rest of it was useless. What's the point of taking fingerprints when you don't have access to a criminal database?

"Isn't it great? I ordered it after you took the case, special delivery. It came this morning. This time when we search Dr. Learner's office, we'll find something for sure!"

"You said something like that on the phone too," I said. "You asked me if I'd found anything."

The color drained out of Sammy's face like water out of a bath. I think he actually had to bite his tongue to keep his mouth shut.

"What did you think I was going to find?"

Most of the time, the best way to get someone to talk is to make them sit in silence. Especially someone like Sammy. I waited and watched as the wheels spun in his head. I only had to count prime numbers up to seventeen before he cracked.

"I didn't mean anything specific," he stammered. "I just

wanted to know if you found any clues, that's all. Like a ransom note or something like that." Sammy had been reading too many detective books. He looked at me out of the corner of his eye to see if I was buying it. I wasn't. So Sammy kept on trying.

"Or maybe you found something about his research, or where he hid it. I don't know. I just wanted to help."

"Wait, back up," I said, as the car braked suddenly as someone swerved into traffic in front of us. I checked the window again for the silver Mercedes, but it still wasn't there. Then I turned back to Sammy. "I knew about Dr. Learner's secret briefcase from Graham Davidson. How did you know?"

Sammy froze, a total rabbit in the headlights. He licked his lips.

"I don't know, *maybe* he hid it. If no one can find it, it must be hidden somewhere, right?" he backpedaled furiously.

"Hidden or it never existed at all," I said. I was getting tired of Sammy not telling the whole truth. The worst part was, I couldn't figure out why he was lying. Or what he was hiding. I knew he wanted to find Dr. Learner, so why wouldn't he tell me everything he knew?

I gave Sammy one more hard look, but I knew I wasn't going to get anything else out of him.

"All right, all right." I held up my hands. There was no point in arguing with Sammy if I didn't have any facts to back up my theory.

Sammy watched me. His face was tense, but it softened when he realized I was done asking questions. He pulled his backpack onto his lap and spent the rest of the journey examining the car's leather interior with his mail-order magnifying glass.

(17

WHEN WE FINALLY arrived at Delgado Industries, the chauffeur made his way through the parking lot and toward the back of the building. He parked and came around the side, opening the door for Sammy. I let myself out.

"My dad's private entrance is back here. I told him we were coming this morning. He'll let us in."

Sammy led me up a few steps to a large metal door with a keypad lock and intercom. He pressed the buzzer.

"Dad, it's me."

The door clicked and Sammy pulled with all his strength. It came open, but so slowly it was like watching the glaciers recede. I grabbed on and helped.

Mr. Delgado sat back in his swivel chair with his legs propped up on his desk. Across from him in a low metal chair sat a very young, very eager-looking reporter. She must have been a new recruit. Mr. Delgado was on the phone, and she didn't even have her Dictaphone running. Dad would have had a fit. I didn't know who was on the other end of the line, but Mr. Delgado looked very pleased with what they were saying.

"Well, I'm glad you feel that way," he said after a long pause. "No, I completely understand. We wouldn't want you to sign anything without being completely sure. Bad business practice."

The reporter looked at us and then back at Mr. Delgado. I guess she didn't think we were worth talking to. I shrugged and followed Sammy to a hard leather couch on the other side of the room. She obviously wasn't a crime reporter; she would have pounced on us in a heartbeat. Maybe she was someone from the lifestyle section?

Mr. Delgado's office was a large, airy room. One wall was made entirely of glass, which surprised me since it had looked solid from the other side. Now I could see Sammy's chauffeur reading the paper in the front seat of the town car. No one coming to visit Mr. Delgado would ever have the element of surprise.

"It's insulated one-way glass," Sammy said when he saw me staring at the window. "You can see out, but not in. They invented it here."

I had to admit, I was impressed. It was hard not to be. The whole room was designed to inspire awe. A large abstract painting hung on the wall behind Mr. Delgado, bold splashes of paint arcing across the canvas. A gold-and-mahogany nameplate that read DR. SAMUEL G. DELGADO, PHD sat on the front of his desk. It looked brand-new. He must have ordered it as soon as he heard the university was giving him an honorary degree. I wondered how long he'd been waiting to be able to call himself a doctor.

"Dad likes to entertain clients here; that's why he's got the separate door. He uses it if he's making deals with people he doesn't want the competition to know about. That way they can come in and out without anyone knowing. And he's the only one with a key to his office, so no one can interrupt him. My dad's really smart about business." Sammy puffed out his chest.

"I guess that's why he's in charge," I said.

Mr. Delgado hung up the phone and turned to the reporter.

"I'm so sorry, Maria, but as you can see I'm a very busy man. Now, where were we?"

Maria smiled. "You were telling me about when you first decided to open Delgado Industries."

"Of course, now let me see. It all started back when I was at grad school . . ."

It looked like Mr. Delgado would be talking for a while. I didn't like waiting around, but until I got the keys to Dr. Learner's lab, I wasn't going anywhere. I stood up and started exploring the room.

There was a large media cabinet next to the couch. It was made of black lacquer with shelves running up the left-hand side and a large-screen TV in the middle. A silver tray filled with glass bottles and cut-crystal glasses sat at eye level, and above it were various books and small sculptures.

I opened the drawers of the cabinet absentmindedly. More bottles of alcohol and packs of cigars wrapped tightly in plastic, a pack of batteries, and a remote control. Several hand-labeled DVDs—presentations for investors, probably. In the back of the drawer with the DVDs was a small stack of mirrors. They were perfectly square, about four inches wide, with no rim or frame around the outside. They looked like they belonged inside a piece of machinery, like a telescope or laser. They seemed so out of place in Mr. Delgado's designer office that I picked up the stack to get a closer look.

"What are you doing?"

I turned around.

Mr. Delgado wasn't smiling and looking pleased with himself anymore.

"Sorry. I can't resist drawers." I held out the mirrors. "Were these Dr. Learner's? They look like they might go in one of those machines in his office."

Mr. Delgado smoothed his hand across his hair, glanced at the reporter, and put his smile back on.

"Yes. Adrian asked me to special-order those a few days ago, before he went missing. I never got the chance to give them to him."

He didn't move from his chair, and he didn't say anything, but I knew he wanted me to put the mirrors down. It was strange. The mirrors were easily the cheapest things in his office, so why did Mr. Delgado have to special-order them? And why did he look so jumpy?

"So, I hear you got a doctorate yesterday," I said, trying to lighten the mood. I turned around and put the mirrors back in the drawer. Well, all of them except for one. I slipped the top mirror into my bag as I turned around.

"Yes, yes. It was quite an honor. Maria here is doing a profile on me for the alumni magazine."

That explained why she wasn't digging for dirt. She was writing 100-percent puff.

"Maria, this is my son, Samuel Junior, and his friend Alice Jones. They're helping me look into the disappearance of my top scientist. I'm sure you've heard about it. Dr. Learner went to the University of Pennsylvania too."

Maria nodded sympathetically, but I could see her eyes glittering. She was thinking she'd just found the perfect angle for her profile on Mr. Delgado. Something to spice it up. I jabbed Sammy in the ribs with my elbow so he'd hurry up and get us out of there. Mr. Delgado looked like he was about to launch into some long-winded story about how wonderful he was, and I didn't want to get stuck as the audience.

"Actually, Adrian and I were at grad school together. In a lot of ways, he was my inspiration." Mr. Delgado handed Maria a framed photo from his desk. "There's me and Adrian before we graduated. We always dreamed about doing research together." His voice trailed off.

I looked over Maria's shoulder. The picture showed Dr. Learner and Mr. Delgado about thirty years ago, younger and with more hair. The two of them were onstage and Dr. Learner was pulling a rabbit out of a hat.

"That was from the Physics Department talent show. We won first prize that year." He gave the photo a wistful smile and then laughed. "I remember one time—"

"Dad!" Sammy cut him off. I got the feeling Sammy heard a lot of stories about Mr. Delgado's glory days. Either that or he sensed me gearing up for another elbow jab.

"Yes, Sammy? What was it you wanted to see me about? You wanted to have another look at Dr. Learner's lab?"

I ignored the look he gave the reporter over our heads. A look that said, *Aren't kids the cutest?*

"That's right," I answered. "I just want to check a few things." Mr. Delgado pulled open his desk drawers and rooted around until he found his keys. I waited until he put them in my hand before I continued, "I also thought I should let you know, I went to Dr. Learner's apartment yesterday."

"You did?" Mr. Delgado looked a little surprised. So maybe the silver Mercedes wasn't his after all. "And did you find anything important there?"

"Not exactly," I said. "I was just wondering . . ." I realized there was no nice way to ask it, so I just blurted out the question. "Well, you were friends with Dr. Learner. Was his place always such a dump?"

Mr. Delgado laughed. "She doesn't sugarcoat things, does she?" he said to Maria, smiling again. Then he turned back to me. "The truth is, Adrian has always been all about the science. When he's working on an experiment, he can go for weeks without going home. He'll sleep on the floor here, or in his car. And he's been so busy on this project, especially after his breakthrough six months ago. It doesn't surprise me that his place was a mess."

I nodded. Sammy looked miserable.

"Is that everything?" Mr. Delgado asked.

"No. After I left, there were some people from the FBI watching the apartment. They stopped me and asked me some questions. I told them what I know. I'm sorry if you didn't want me to, but I didn't feel like lying to the federal government."

"No," Mr. Delgado said. "That wouldn't do at all. No, you

did fine, better than fine. I'm very pleased with what you've done so far."

"But I haven't done anything," I said.

"But I'm sure you are making great progress. Sammy keeps me updated. Now if you'll excuse me, I think Maria has some more questions she wants to ask before we tour the facility."

It occurred to me that Mr. Delgado had planned for me and Sammy to run into his tame reporter. It was exactly the kind of publicity he wanted. It kept Dr. Learner's disappearance in the paper, but it also made Mr. Delgado look pretty good. The kind of great guy who lets his son and friends play at being detectives. But I wasn't playing. If I was looking into the case at all, then I was looking into the case for real. I thanked Mr. Delgado for his time and said good-bye. I wanted to have another look at Dr. Learner's office as soon as possible.

"Oh, one more thing," I said as I stood in the office doorway. "I've noticed a car following me. I think it might be someone from Chronos R & D."

Mr. Delgado stood up quickly, knocking his state-of-the-art swivel chair backward into the wall.

"Chronos? Are you sure? Why do you think it's them?"

I didn't think it was a good idea to tell Mr. Delgado how my dad had hacked into Dr. Learner's emails. So I told him I heard the name from the FBI.

"This is very serious. Thank you for letting me know." He picked up the phone, nodding an apology to Maria. "Alice, if you see those men again, don't talk to them, don't tell them anything. Just call for help right away. They are not nice people and I don't want you to get hurt."

It wasn't what he said that scared me. It was the way he said it, like he was afraid of them.

"Sammy, you make sure Alice gets home safely."

Then again, if he trusted Sammy to keep me safe, how scary could they really be?

I spent the next hour searching Dr. Learner's office, trying to see if there was a blind spot I'd missed. I was certain there had to be another way out of that office. A way that got Dr. Learner past the security cameras. Sammy stood at the doorway, like he was some kind of bodyguard. I didn't know what he thought he'd do if trouble actually did show up.

There was no blind spot. No hidden alcove. Nowhere Dr. Learner could have hidden in that room when Graham Davidson came to check on him. I even stood on the work surface and checked the ceiling to see if Dr. Learner could have crawled out through an air vent. But it was no good.

"I got nothing," I said to Sammy. "Let's get out of here. I feel like my brain is going to implode."

Sammy walked me back through his dad's office and out into the parking lot. Mr. Delgado was gone, probably giving Maria a five-star tour of the building. The driver was waiting for us. He'd gotten out of the car when we'd left the building and was holding the door open for Sammy by the time we made it to the car.

"Can you take Alice home for me?"

It must have been weird for the driver, taking orders from a kid. He looked about forty-five.

I climbed into the car. Sammy didn't follow me.

"Aren't you coming?"

"I've got my own job, remember?"

I stared at Sammy blankly.

"You know," he said, leaning closer and shielding his mouth so the driver couldn't see. "The device that was on the security camera. The one that might be a clue to how Dr. Learner got out of his office. I'm gonna search for it while my dad's giving the tour."

He stood back, pleased with himself. I felt a pang of guilt as I remembered sending Sammy on that rainbow frog chase. But he looked so happy I didn't have the heart to tell him to give up.

"I'll call you later," Sammy said, and started to close the door. He shut it halfway and then opened it again. "Do you think we should have a secret password for when we call each other? Just in case?"

I looked at Sammy, dumbfounded. That kid read way too many spy novels.

Sammy waited for a moment, but when he realized I wasn't going to answer he just shrugged. "Well, think about it," he said, and slammed the door.

(18

ON THE WAY home, I found out that the chauffeur's name was Ellis. He had a wife and three kids and obviously didn't get the chance to talk to a lot of people. By the time we got to my house, I knew about 80 percent of Ellis's life story. He parked the car, and I climbed out. I liked Ellis, but not enough to stick around and hear the last 20 percent.

"Thanks for the ride." I ran up the steps before he had a chance to reply.

I gave Ellis one more quick wave good-bye, then I turned around and froze.

The door was open.

Not unlocked. Open.

It wasn't even latched. I could see a small slice of kitchen between the edge of the door and the frame. It was propped open by the mat Dad insisted we wipe our feet on. It must have been kicked up when someone left in a hurry. At least I hoped they had left. Deep gouges cut into the wood where somebody had used a crowbar to pry the door open.

My hands were shaking as I pulled out my phone.

"Come on, Dad. Pick up."

I pushed the door open slowly. Someone had been through our house, and they hadn't been careful about it. All of the kitchen cupboards were open, and the couch cushions were on the floor. The few family pictures that were still hanging on the walls were crooked. I stepped inside.

"Hello?" Dad's voice on the other end of the phone made me jump.

"Dad, someone broke into our house."

"What? Are you OK? Where are you?"

"I'm fine. I just got home. I don't think they're still here."

"Get out of the house. And call the police. I'm coming."

"But Dad, what about Della?"

"I'll call her. But she said something about some extra vocal coaching at the university. I think she's there. Just get out."

I did what he said. I got out of the house and called the police. Whoever I talked to kept telling me to calm down. Eventually, they said they'd send someone over. When I hung up, there was a text from Dad saying Della was fine. She was at her music lesson in the city. I was so relieved I almost cried.

I waited on the other side of the street for the police, just staring at the door to our house. It was the way I'd stared at my closet door at night, back when I was a kid and still believed in monsters. As if the second I stopped watching, the door would open and something evil would come out. It was ninety degrees in the shade, and I was shaking like a leaf.

It was the men in the silver car. They were from Chronos R & D. They had to be. And that's why they didn't follow me that morning. They were waiting until I left the house. I hugged my messenger bag to my chest. They were looking for the Delgado file. Police sirens sounded in the distance and then moved closer. I don't think I've ever heard anything so sweet.

The squad car pulled up, its blue lights flashing, and two officers climbed out. A young man and a middle-aged woman.

"I'm Officer Ross, this is Officer Tulley. Are you the one who reported the break-in?" the woman asked. Her dark hair was pulled back tight against her skull, but her eyes were warm. I started breathing again. Officer Tulley stayed next to the car. He looked like the kind of guy who wasn't comfortable dealing with kids.

I nodded and pointed to our house. "It's that one."

"Is anyone inside?"

"I don't know. I didn't go all the way in. No one's come out, though."

"OK, you stay here while we clear the building. Are your parents here?"

"My dad's on his way."

I watched the two of them go into our house.

Put your hand on a hot stove for a minute, and it seems like an hour. Sit with a pretty girl for an hour, and it seems like a minute. That's relativity. That's how Einstein explained it, anyway. I finally understood what he meant. Every second that I stood there alone felt like a year. Putting my hand on a hot stove would have been a picnic.

My dad pulled up about a minute after the cops went in, but it felt like a lot longer. He parked on the wrong side of the street, pulling up onto the curb so he didn't block traffic completely. He was out of the car and had me in a bear hug in two steps.

"Are you OK?" Dad kept his arm around my shoulders and held me tight against his side.

"Yeah. The cops just went inside. What about Della?"

"She's fine. She's on her way home too."

Officer Tulley stuck his head out of the door and waved for us to come over.

"The house is empty." The words should have made me feel better, but they didn't. "Can you see if anything's been stolen?"

Dad started to move, then stopped and turned to me.

"I'm fine. Go check."

Dad looked in his office and then went upstairs to check the bedrooms. My knees felt like jelly.

"Is it all right if I put the cushions back on the couch? I need to sit down."

Officer Tulley shrugged. "Sure. We can't get fingerprints off corduroy anyway."

Dad came back a few minutes later. "I don't think they took anything. The computer's still here, and the TV. Besides that, we don't have anything worth stealing."

"Whoever broke in did a pretty thorough search. Can you think of anything someone might have been looking for?"

Dad shook his head.

"I think I might know." I opened my messenger bag and pulled out the Delgado file. It was everything Delgado had given me, plus the pictures I'd taken at Dr. Learner's apartment and all of my notes. "It doesn't say where Dr. Learner is, but the guys who were following me don't know that."

Dad took the file and flipped through it quickly before handing it to Officer Tulley.

"Wait, someone's been following you? Why didn't you tell me?"

"Sorry, Dad, I meant to tell you about the car this morning, but you were gone before I had a chance. I didn't think they'd break into the house. I mean, there's not even anything in the file really."

"Still, you should have said something."

"This is about that missing scientist?" Officer Ross took the file from Officer Tulley and shook her head. "What a mess."

The door opened again and I jumped, expecting the two men from the Mercedes to storm in and rip the file out of Officer Ross's hands. But it was just another group of officers wearing dark-blue shirts with CRIME SCENE TEAM written on the back instead of the regular police uniform. Officer Tulley went to show them where to dust for fingerprints.

Officer Ross ignored them and kept talking. "We'll have a patrol car drive by every hour tonight. There's a chance they might try to come back if they didn't get what they were after the first time. If I were you, I'd find somewhere safe to keep that file. And try to let people know it isn't here anymore. Make sure you use the dead bolt and the chain. They had an easy time popping the door open because the only lock used was the Yale lock."

That was Della. She lived in an apartment building in New York with its own security. She probably just let the door shut behind her when she left this morning. I kept reminding her she needed to lock the dead bolt, but she was used to doing things her own way.

"Call us if you see anything suspicious," Officer Ross said. She handed Dad the file and gave each of us a card. "That's my direct number."

And with that, Officer Ross and Officer Tulley left. Dad and I stood on the front steps for a long time after they drove away. I don't think either of us wanted to go back inside, especially while the Crime Scene Team were there. It didn't feel like home anymore. Those men had broken it.

I counted up in primes and tried to figure out my next move. It took me until eighty-nine to calm down enough to think straight. Everything Sammy had said made me believe that Dr. Learner had nothing to do with Chronos. If he was on the run, it was because he was hiding from those jerks, not working for them. I kept counting. I was in triple digits now: 101, 103, 107, 109. If Chronos thought they could use me to find Dr. Learner, they had another thing coming. 113. I was going to find Dr. Learner first. 127. I was going to keep him safe for Sammy. 131. And I was going to make Chronos R & D sorry they'd ever messed with a Jones.

I could tell by the way Dad was tapping his fingers against my shoulder that he was thinking the exact same thing.

(19

WE FINALLY WENT back inside when Della came home. A taxi pulled up and Della got out, demanding Dad pay the driver.

"Are you OK? I came back as fast as I could, but tons of the roads on the university campus are closed because of that stupid new science building they're constructing. Did they take anything?" She was wearing a long embroidered dress and had sunglasses on top of her head. My sunglasses. I knew I should be happy that she was all right, but all I felt was angry. I bit my tongue and let Dad do the talking.

"It doesn't look like it," Dad said.

"I'd better check. You might not notice if they took some of my stuff."

When we stepped back inside, I didn't recognize the place. Every smooth surface was covered in a fine layer of gray powder, like someone had crawled up a chimney and sneezed.

"Ah, we're just about done here," said a bald man who I assumed was the chief technician. "We just need the prints of the people who live here for elimination purposes."

"That's us," I said.

They took our fingerprints with an electric scanner. First Dad, then Della, then me. As soon as Della had her fingers free, she ran upstairs. She opened the door to my bedroom so hard the house shook.

"Thank you for your cooperation. Here." The technician handed Dad a lint roller. "It's the best way to get the dust off."

Dad shut the door behind the Crime Scene Team and locked it. It didn't make me feel any safer. I could see daylight through the gouges the crowbar had left in the frame. I didn't realize I was shaking until Dad wrapped his arm around me. I couldn't tell if it was because I was scared or angry. Probably a little of both.

I tilted my head back against my dad's chest. He looked tired and worried, his skin pale and stretched tight across his cheekbones. I hadn't seen him look like that for a long time.

Upstairs Della was getting louder and louder, banging drawers open and closed. I thought I heard her move the bed. I glared at the ceiling. If Della had remembered to lock the dead bolt, none of this would have happened.

Dad looked up at the ceiling, then back down at me.

"All right, Alice. Give me the file." He let me go and held out his hand.

"What?"

"The file those men came looking for. You're off this case. I'll call Mr. Delgado and tell him you can't help him anymore. Why didn't you tell me there were men following you? What were you thinking?"

"But Dad," I started, but before I could explain, the door to my room slammed open and Della came tearing back down the stairs.

"They're gone," she wailed. "They stole my lucky earrings. Call the police, get them back here right now."

"Della, calm down," Dad said. He strode across the room to where Della was taking deep breaths, like she was trying not to hyperventilate. "Are you sure they're missing? Maybe they're on the floor."

"I'm not an idiot. I checked the floor. I checked everywhere. I had them laid out on the table ready to wear tomorrow. And now they're gone. I can't believe this is happening to me. I need those earrings for my callback."

"Sweetheart, calm down. I'll get you another pair of earrings. What did they look like?"

Della shot him a look so cold it could stop global warming.

"They were diamond studs. Mom bought them for me

when I got my first role on Broadway. They are my LUCKY earrings. You can't just go out and buy another pair. You don't understand. You never understand."

Della turned away from our dad in disgust. And then she saw me.

"This is all your fault," she said, jamming her finger into my chest.

"My fault? I'm not the one who forgot to lock the dead bolt this morning."

"Maybe if you had a normal hobby and didn't go running around looking for criminals, people wouldn't break into our house."

"Oh, shut up, Delores," I snapped back.

Della took a deep breath and turned to Dad. She hated when I called her by her full name.

"I'm not talking to her. Call the police and tell them to come back. I need those earrings for my callback tomorrow."

I wasn't going to let her get away with that. "Stop making this all about you, Della. Why don't you just go to Italy with Mom already? You'd be happier there anyway."

"Alice!" Dad yelled.

Della took off up the stairs.

Great, I thought, as the door to my room slammed again. *Where am I supposed to run off to?*

Dad scowled down at me. He's a good foot taller than me, and at that moment he really loomed.

"Don't you move," he said. "I'm going to talk to your sister, and when I come back down I want that file and everything you have on Dr. Learner's disappearance. Do you understand?"

I nodded. I understood, all right. But if Dad thought I was going to roll over just like that, he didn't know me as well as he thought he did.

As soon as he was out of sight, I grabbed the file and took it into Dad's office. I guessed I had about ten minutes before he came back down, more if Della decided to turn on the water-works. The computer would take forever to boot up, but fortunately I didn't need the computer. Dad had one of those four-in-one printer/fax/copy/scanner machines. I copied the entire file twice. I hid one copy by putting it back in the printer, at the bottom of the paper tray. I stuffed the other copy into the waistband of my shorts. I put the originals back in the folder and ran into the living room just as Dad came back down the stairs.

"Your sister is very upset."

I said nothing. He sighed.

"She's on the phone with your mom."

Well, that was just great. Now Mom would be mad at me too.

"Look, Alice." Dad took his glasses off and looked at me wearily. "I know it hasn't always been easy living apart from your sister. But it's really important that you two get along. Your mom and I won't always be around. I thought this summer would be a chance for the two of you to reconnect. You should go and make peace with her."

Dad looked at me hopefully. But if he thought I was going to go upstairs and apologize, he was going to be disappointed. Della was just as much to blame as I was, and this time she could apologize first.

"Fine," he sighed. "You'll deal with it on your own. I got it. Now"—he put his glasses back on and held out his hand—"the file."

"But, Dad, it's got all my notes and ideas. I'll be more careful. I swear. And I'm close to figuring something out. I can feel it."

"Tough cookies, kiddo." He wiggled the fingers of his waiting hand.

I made a show of reluctantly handing him the originals.

"What are you going to do with them?" I asked.

"I'll take them to work. There's security there, so your notes will be safe if anyone comes after them."

"Dad?"

"Don't worry. I'll use all the information in my exposé on Chronos R & D. I don't care how long legal takes to approve it.

No one breaks into my home and gets away with it. They won't know what hit them."

I smiled.

Dad smiled back at me. "Besides, once I print whatever is in here, there'll be no reason for anyone to come back and try to steal it." He tucked the file under his arm and held his hand out again.

"Now give me the other one."

"Other what?"

"Alice Jones, you're my daughter. Don't think I don't know what you were doing in my office. Now give me the copy you made."

We stared at each other, hard. Then I let my eyes fall to the ground.

"Fine." I pulled the dummy file out from under my shirt and handed it over. "But I still think you should let me keep it. I'm so close to figuring it out. And if I find Dr. Learner for you, you could get the story printed even faster. I bet he'd give you an exclusive."

Dad took the file and whacked me softly on the top of my head. "No deal. Any others?"

I shook my head, but Dad did a search anyway. I guess he did know me pretty well. He checked my bag and all my notebooks. He opened all the drawers in his office. He even looked under the black plastic mat that protected the carpet from his office chair.

"I guess this is the only one, then," he said. "Alice, I know you hate to leave anything unsolved, but I'm serious. *This* is serious. For some reason, those men broke the law to try to get that file. Don't go near it. Got it?"

"Yeah, I got it."

"OK, I'm going to take this to the office now, and see if I can get someone to come and fit a new door. I want you to lock up behind me, and put the chain on. Call me if anything happens. I mean *anything*."

I locked the door behind him, dead bolt and chain, and waved through the window as Dad drove away. Then I went back into his office and got the second file out of the printer. I felt a little guilty. But not enough to make me stop. If Dad was going to protect us by writing the truth, I was going to help him figure it out. There was no way I was letting those jerks from Chronos find Dr. Learner and his invisibility suit before I did.

I hole-punched the file and stuck it in the folder where I kept my Goldbach's notes and ideas. I didn't think anyone would look for it there.

(20

I SPENT ANOTHER night on the couch and woke up with a new set of lines decorating my face. Della hadn't actually locked me out of my room, but that was only because the bedroom doors didn't have locks. I snuck in and got clean clothes and pajamas while she was in the shower. Dad had gotten someone to fit an extra set of locks until we could buy a new door. But we all still jumped at every sound out on the street. And every time I jumped I got a little angrier.

Della was practicing her shuffle ball changes upstairs. It sounded like she was practicing them on my face. She'd found the spot on my bedroom floor that was directly over the couch where I was sleeping. She must have moved the desk to do it. I needed coffee.

I pulled on the clothes I'd laid out the night before and used my fingers to brush my hair. Dad was sitting at the counter eating a bowl of cereal and reading the paper.

"Good morning," I said. He didn't respond, and when I looked more closely I could see he had screwed up some paper napkins into makeshift earplugs. The white ends stuck out of his ears like some kind of alien antennae.

I poured myself coffee and cereal and tugged the entertainment section out from under Dad's arm. He jumped.

"Morning, Dad," I said. He had dark circles under his eyes. I guess I wasn't the only one who'd had trouble sleeping. Upstairs, Della stopped tapping.

"Is the band still playing?" He raised his eyes up to the ceiling.

I shook my head.

Dad sighed and pulled out the earplugs, then he took off his glasses and rubbed the bridge of his nose.

"Good morning, sweetheart." He put his glasses back on and passed me a pen so I could do the cryptic quip and the Sudoku. Dad might not have liked giving them up, but he always kept his word. "I need to take Della to her callback today, so I won't be around. Is there anyone you can call to come over? I don't like the idea of you in this house alone."

"You want me to call a babysitter?"

"You know that's not what I mean. If you don't have anyone to come over, why don't you come with us to the audition?"

I knew Dad was trying to help me and Della build bridges, but it was a little too soon for that. I was about to tell him that I didn't think Della would appreciate my company just now when she came down the stairs and told him for me.

"Dad, you can't be serious. I need complete positivity. Alice will poison the atmosphere if she comes."

"Della." Dad's tone was stern, but I didn't want to go to Della's audition any more than she wanted me to be there.

"Don't worry about it, Dad. I'll go to the library. There'll be plenty of people there."

"Fine," he said. "But I'll have my phone with me the entire time. On vibrate," he added quickly when Della opened her mouth. "You call me if you need me, understand?"

"I got it."

"OK. I'm going to grab a quick shower, then I'll take you to the theater. You two be nice to each other."

I think Dad wanted to say something else, probably something about sisters getting along and our special twin connection, but decided against it. Instead he just put his bowl in the sink and went upstairs.

Della sat down at the counter. "Don't look at me, don't talk to me, don't even think about me. Until this audition is over, you do not exist."

"You know, Della, I've tried really hard to make you feel at home here. I gave you my bed and cooked your carbs. Maybe you could just try to be a little understanding. There are other people in the world, you know."

Della sniffed and flipped her beautiful blonde hair at me, but she didn't say a word.

Fine, I thought, *if she wants to play hardball, I can play that way too.*

I looked at Della and very calmly pulled my messenger bag over my head.

"I'm going now. I'll be back tonight. Oh, and Della..." I think she knew what I was going to say before I said it. Maybe we had a twin connection after all. Her hands shot up to cover her ears, but she wasn't fast enough.

"Good luck!"

I grabbed my bike and banged out the door, leaving Della screaming bloody murder over her cornflakes. It was the worst thing you could say to an actress before an audition. But it didn't make me feel any better. The only thing that was going to do that was solving this case. And that meant finding Dr. Learner and proving he got out of that office without using an invisibility suit. Or seeing that suit with my own two eyes.

It was rush hour. The air was full of exhaust fumes and the sound of angry honking. Overhead the sky was dark. It looked like we were due for another storm. I walked my bike along the sidewalk. There was no point in riding when the road was that full. It was like asking someone to run you over. The good thing was, with traffic this bad, it was impossible for the men in the silver Mercedes to follow me. At least, that's what I told myself. But it didn't stop me from jumping when Kevin Jordan shouted at me.

"Hey, Numbers!"

I tried to stuff my heart back into my chest cavity where it belonged and turned around.

"Whoa! Calm down there." Kevin jogged after me, pushing his bike with one hand and dragging Sammy Delgado Jr. with the other. Sammy was holding a large bundle of balloons that trailed behind him.

"What do you want?" I asked. I didn't like being stopped on the side of the street. Every time a silver car drove past, my heart beat a little harder. But none of them was the Mercedes.

"I saw this kid sneaking around outside your house, and I thought you might be up to something interesting."

"I wasn't sneaking, I'm helping Alice on a case," Sammy said, starting loud and then biting back his words when Kevin looked down at him.

"Sorry, Sammy, I'm off the case. Didn't your dad tell you?" I felt bad lying, but I didn't need Sammy shooting his mouth off and word getting back to my dad that I was still looking into things.

Sammy blushed. "I know. Here, I brought you these." He held out the balloons.

"What are these? I'm-sorry-someone-broke-into-your-house balloons?"

He shrugged and nodded at the same time, like a sheepish turtle. I couldn't believe it, but that was Sammy all over. His heart was in the right place. His head was somewhere else altogether. It actually made me smile.

"Wait, someone broke into your house?" Kevin asked. "Why didn't you call me?"

I turned to look at Kevin. I didn't know which was weirder, Sammy's balloons or Kevin's question.

"Why would I call you? I called the police."

We all stood in the middle of the sidewalk, staring at each other. A man in a sharp suit and sneakers shoved past us and swore under his breath. I pulled Kevin and Sammy up against the wall.

"Look, it was a rough night. I don't have time for games right now, so what do both of you want?"

Sammy looked at me and then at Kevin. He made a move like he was going to whisper in my ear.

"Whoa there," I said, pushing him gently back. "Kevin knows about the case. You don't need to play spy."

Sammy looked at me like I'd stabbed him.

"Fine," he said, sulking. "It's about that thing you asked me to look for. I couldn't find it. I checked the whole building. Sorry."

"What thing?" Kevin asked. We were all standing over a subway grate. Somewhere below us a train went by and the hot, stale air blew up. It felt like a dog's hot breath on my legs.

"Sammy, it's not a secret," I said. I was pretty sure it didn't even matter. "There was a metal clip on the security camera in one of the photos. It wasn't there when I went to look at the real thing. Sammy was trying to find it for me."

Sammy puffed out his chest like a peacock. "That's right. I checked Dad's office, and Dr. Learner's lab. And I snuck into Graham Davidson's office while he was on his lunch break. I even checked all of the conference rooms upstairs. But it wasn't anywhere."

"Someone probably threw it out," Kevin said. "Did you check the trash cans?"

Sammy went quiet. For a minute I thought the poor kid was going to cry. Watching him made my chest ache.

"I need to go," he said. "I just remembered there's something I need to do. Not this. Something else. I'll see you later."

He shoved the balloons into my hand and ran off, looking backward and tripping over his feet. I was pretty sure that the black town car was parked somewhere nearby. Sammy didn't seem like a big walker.

"Weird kid," Kevin said.

"Look who's talking."

Traffic was starting to move again, and the sidewalks were

clearing. I climbed on my bike and started to pedal toward the library.

"So, a break-in, huh? That must have been pretty scary. Are you OK?"

"I'm fine." I didn't feel like sharing. Especially not with Kevin. Not after I told him all that stuff about Della and Dad and how I felt about my family. I was playing it safe and keeping my mouth shut.

"Is your dad OK?"

"He's fine."

"What about your sister? Doesn't she have her audition today?"

I squeezed the brakes so hard my back wheel popped off the ground. I lost hold of the balloons and they floated up, seven red circles disappearing into the heavy gray sky. I didn't even try to catch them.

"Why are you following me?"

"I'm not following you. We're just going in the same direction." Kevin showed me his most angelic smile.

"I'm going to the library," I said. "Where are you going?"

"I'm going to the library too."

"You're going to the library? During the summer? You?"

"Yep. Look up and watch the pigs flying."

(21

KEVIN NEEDED TO fill in a library card application, so I left him at the mercy of the surliest librarian this side of the Ben Franklin Bridge and disappeared into the stacks.

I followed the Dewey decimal system to the 510s, the math section. It was quiet there and I liked the books. My favorite spot was a window ledge between Arithmetic (513) and Analytical Geometry (516). Other, taller buildings had been built up around the library so the window looked across an alley onto a brick wall. It made that corner of the library feel like a secret hiding place, somewhere in the city where no one could see me. Dust motes speckled the air, catching the summer sun. I checked one more time to make sure no one had followed me, and then I got out my Goldbach's Conjecture folder.

The mirror I'd taken from Mr. Delgado's office was still at the bottom of my bag, a thin layer of pencil dust clouding the surface. I wiped it clean on the front of my shirt and tucked it into the plastic pocket at the front of the binder. Then I flipped through the pages looking for where my copy of the Delgado file started. Dad might have told me to leave the case alone. But that was like trying to make one plus one equal five. Still, I wasn't stupid. I wasn't going to go running around the city searching for Dr. Learner. I had all the information in the file on my lap. If I found a clue or figured out a lead, I'd call Mr. Delgado. He could handle it from there. I'd make sure he gave Dad an exclusive story too.

I paused for a moment on the last page of my notes on Goldbach's Conjecture. I'd planned to spend a quiet summer working on a proof. I'd also planned to spend a couple of nights sleeping in my own bed. That hadn't worked out for me either. I turned the page over with a sigh and started reviewing the case.

I tapped the end of my pen against my cheek, counting as I thought. I was sure the key to the case was the way Dr. Learner had disappeared. If I could just figure out the trick, the rest of the equation would fall into place. Unlike Graham Davidson, I refused to just believe that Dr. Learner had built an invisibility suit. Not until I saw some proof. Then again, I didn't know Dr. Learner. And everyone did say he was a genius. I shook my head. No, even if Dr. Learner was the smartest guy on the planet and he had built a working suit, the case still didn't make any sense. Why would he use it to disappear? What was the point?

I turned to a clean page and started writing down all the possible reasons I could think of for staging an impossible disappearance.

Maybe he was trying to hide from someone. I could understand that. I might not have seen the men in the silver Mercedes that morning, but they were out there somewhere. Being able to disappear sounded pretty nice. Still, inventing a multimillion-dollar invisibility suit was a pretty drastic way to make your escape.

Maybe he was trying to prove that the device worked. But if he wanted to do that, he could just show someone. Maybe he *had* shown someone. Sammy seemed pretty sure that the suit was real. Then again, Sammy probably still believed in the tooth fairy. But if the suit didn't exist, what was this all about? And how had Dr. Learner pulled that Houdini from his office? It was a classic paradox, leading me around and around in a strange loop. I closed my eyes. Paradoxes were fine in theory, but this was the real world. There had to be a logical explanation. I just hadn't found it yet.

I took out my phone and flipped through the pictures I'd taken at Dr. Learner's apartment, hoping to spot something

I'd missed. But no matter how hard I looked at the scraps of equations taped to Dr. Learner's refrigerator or the cluttered floor, nothing jumped out at me. I stared the longest at the photo I'd taken in Dr. Learner's bedroom. There was something about that one clean square of space that bothered me. But I couldn't put my finger on what it was.

"There you are. This place is huge." Kevin came around the corner of the stacks, speaking way too loudly for a library. I shoved my phone back into my pocket.

"Quiet. This is a library, you know."

Kevin rolled his eyes. "I'm not actually an idiot," he said.

"You could have fooled me." I said it under my breath, but we were in a library. Under your breath is the same as shouting. I cringed. "Sorry."

If the apology surprised me, it gave Kevin a heart attack.

He staggered backward, clutching at his chest and gasping for air, sliding down the shelves into a twitching heap on the floor.

I laughed in spite of myself. It started as a giggle and then it got out of hand. I laughed so hard the patrolling librarian came to shush me. Me. Even then I couldn't stop. Kevin looked worried, and the thought of Kevin Jordan worrying about me made me laugh even harder.

Kevin grabbed my arm, scooped up my stuff, and pulled me out of the stacks. He dragged me past the librarian and all the staring library patrons. Maybe it was their shocked looks, or the fact that I was running out of air, or maybe it was the tightness of Kevin's fingers around my wrist that shook me back to my senses. Maybe it was all three. But I knew I needed to get a grip.

I took some deep breaths and counted prime numbers. When that didn't work, I switched to the Fibonacci sequence. By the time we got outside (and I'd gotten to $F_{14} = 377$) I'd managed to calm down. I bent over, bracing my hands on my knees, and tried to catch my breath. My stomach ached. I couldn't remember the last time I'd laughed that hard.

"Here." Kevin handed me a bottle of water from his bag and I gulped it down.

"Thanks."

I sat down on the marble steps. The storm was getting closer; I could almost feel the weight of the water in the clouds pressing down on us. I scanned the street; still no silver Mercedes. Most of me felt relieved, but a small part wondered: If they weren't following me, where were they? And what were they up to? They hadn't just given up, I was sure of that.

Kevin sat down next to me. "That's the first time I've seen you laugh."

"Really?" I thought back over the year. He was probably right. School wasn't exactly a comedy club.

"You only ever smile when you're writing in that." He

nodded toward my Goldbach's Conjecture folder. "What's in there?"

I looked at Kevin and tried to imagine a world where I could explain Goldbach's Conjecture without a blank look or a snide remark. I could almost see it. All that laughing must have shaken something loose in my brain.

"It's just a math problem I like working on. It's not important."

Kevin raised an eyebrow like he didn't believe me, but he didn't push it.

"So why did you come to the library today?" I changed the subject.

"Ah. I needed your help. With this."

Kevin pulled a thick stack of papers out of his bag. They were stapled in the top corner and slightly damp from where his water bottle must have leaked. "Principal Chase wasn't happy about me running off without seeing her on the last day of school."

"I can see how that might have upset her." I wasn't sure where Kevin was going with this, but I had a feeling it involved asking me for a favor.

"She went mental. She called my house. Luckily, I got to the phone before my parents. It took everything I had to calm her down." The idea of Kevin charming Principal Chase almost made me start laughing all over again. "She said if I turned in all of these workbooks before summer detention starts next week, I don't have to go."

"So?" I said. "Fill them in."

"I need to get over ninety percent." He looked at me, practically batting his eyelashes.

"You must be joking. I'm not doing your homework for you."

"Aw, come on. I didn't say that. Just help me. It's your fault, you know. If I hadn't run off trying to save you, I wouldn't be in this mess."

"Why didn't you just tell her what happened?"

"What, about the two gorillas in black suits who shoved you into a car and drove off? I tried. She didn't believe a word of it. Come on, you're smart. Just help me out here. I'm an idiot, remember?"

I looked at the workbooks and back at Kevin.

"Come on," Kevin said. "I'll buy you a pretzel."

"Fine. I'll help. But I'm not giving you the answers."

I helped Kevin with his math workbook, and it was like pulling teeth.

"It says right here, *Show your work!* Half of the marks are for showing your work."

"Who cares how you get there if you get the right answer?"

"Because math isn't all about the answer. It's about the process. If you just write down the answer, you might as well have just looked it up in the back of the book."

"Wait, the answers are in the back of the book?" Kevin flipped through the pages and then sighed. "I knew it was too good to be true."

I pressed the heels of my hands against my eyes. We were getting nowhere fast. I could understand if Kevin wanted the answers so he could work backward and figure out the solutions, but he didn't. He didn't get that half the joy of math is figuring out *how* to solve the problem.

I stopped.

It was me all over. How had Dr. Learner escaped? The problem had taken up so much space in my brain, I hadn't stopped to think about anything else. About the real problem. Where was Dr. Learner now? I didn't need to solve the problem of Dr. Learner's mysterious disappearance. I needed to solve the problem of Dr. Learner's current location. That's what the men from Chronos R & D were doing. They hadn't just given up following me. They'd probably found a new lead, something I hadn't thought of yet. And I refused to let them find Dr. Learner first. This was *my* case, not theirs.

"Kevin, you're a genius," I said. He was too shocked to reply.

I got out my phone and did a search for Dr. Adrian Learner. Most of the results were news reports of his disappearance. I saw the one my father had written near the top of the page. He'd be happy about that.

"I don't want news, I want a biography." I scrolled down. There.

It was an article from the University of Pennsylvania's alumni magazine: *Penn's Science Success Stories*. Dr. Learner and Mr. Delgado were both heavily featured. I skimmed through the page.

"He won the Beakman Fellowship . . ."

"Whoa, check out those sideburns!" Kevin pointed to a picture of a young Dr. Learner in a lab coat with what looked like a group of other graduate students. They were standing in front of a large window in one of the university buildings, the Philadelphia skyline sparkling in the background. I looked more closely. Standing next to Dr. Learner was a younger, skinnier version of Mr. Delgado.

> Dr. Adrian Learner will join his former classmate
> Mr. Samuel Delgado to help us open the new
> Delgado-Learner Science Building in September.
> The building features offices for new science
> faculty, eight classrooms, and four state-of-the-
> art laboratories.

And there it was, finally. A lead.

Everyone I'd talked to said Dr. Learner was a brilliant man, absolutely devoted to his research. He'd never willingly leave in the middle of a project. That's why Sammy was so worried. But what if there was somewhere he could keep working in secret?

(22

"THERE," I SAID. "That has to be it. A lab at the new science building."

"What, you think he's at the university? Wouldn't someone have already checked there?"

"The building's been under construction all year. It's still not open. Yesterday, Della was complaining about the roads on campus being closed because of it. And Graham Davidson said Dr. Learner hated to leave his experiments. If he disappeared of his own free will, he'd want to be somewhere he could keep working. People were looking for places he might be living, places with beds. But Dr. Learner would sleep on his office floor if he needed to. And it would be really easy for him to hide on campus. There's lots of people going in and out, so he'd just look like another professor."

I dialed Mr. Delgado's cell number.

"Hello?"

It was Andrew, Mr. Delgado's Personal Secretary with capital letters.

"Andrew, it's Alice Jones."

"Ah, Miss Jones. How can I help you?" It was hard to hear him over the people talking in the background and the faint sound of a piano.

"I need to talk to Mr. Delgado."

"I'm afraid Mr. Delgado is busy at the moment. We're having a little celebration." He slurred his words a bit, and I wondered if Andrew had had a few too many sips of champagne. If so, it must have been some party.

"What are you celebrating over there?"

"It isn't official yet, but it looks like we've won the contract. We'll make the official announcement after we sign the papers tomorrow. It's a real coup for Delgado Industries."

I was surprised Andrew didn't try to cover up his mistake. I knew Delgado Industries was trying to win that forty-million-dollar contract with the government, but only because Dad snooped through Dr. Learner's emails. But I guessed if they were announcing it tomorrow, it didn't really matter. I had bigger things to worry about anyway.

"Right, well, good for you," I said. "But I still need to talk to Mr. Delgado. I think I might have a lead on Dr. Learner."

"Really," Andrew said, "I'm so sorry, he can't come to the

phone. But I'll take a message and pass it to him as soon as possible."

"Fine, tell him I think Dr. Learner might be hiding out at the University of Pennsylvania. In the new science building he bought them."

"New science building. Right. I will let him know," Andrew said, and suppressed a hiccup.

"Make sure you tell him right away. I think those men from Chronos R & D are still looking for Dr. Learner."

Andrew chuckled to himself the way adults do when kids are "acting grown-up." It made my hair stand on end.

"I'll be sure to tell Mr. Delgado right away," he said. Then he hung up on me.

I was not filled with confidence.

"So, is that it?" Kevin asked. "Hey, if you get that reward money, will you buy me a new bike? My brakes are busted."

I didn't like it. Mr. Delgado would be stuck at that party all afternoon. Andrew might not even remember to give him the message. And for all I knew, the men from the Mercedes were already on their way.

I called my dad and paced up and down, counting steps while the phone rang. I'd gotten to nineteen when Dad's phone transferred me to voice mail.

"Della must be in the middle of her audition," I said as I hung up.

I started down the steps to where I'd locked my bike.

"Wait, what are you doing?" Kevin asked.

"I'm going to the university. Those Chronos guys might have figured it out already."

He stood at the top of the steps staring while I undid the chain and swung my leg over the seat.

"Well," I called up to him, "are you coming or what?"

Kevin shook himself awake, and then jumped down the steps. "Fine, but if we do find him, you definitely owe me a bike."

We rode through the city in silence. I kept picturing Sammy back at Delgado Industries, hunting through the trash. He might be hiding something, but he was serious about solving the case. He'd probably climb into a Dumpster if he thought it would bring back Dr. Learner. It was strange—a week ago I couldn't stand Sammy, but now I didn't want to let him down.

I pedaled faster, and Kevin kept up.

We crossed the Schuylkill River on Walnut Street and pedaled into the heart of the university.

The Delgado-Learner Science Building was on the west side of the campus. Half of the building was hidden by scaffolding, but the parts I could see seemed to be finished. Two young elm trees flanked the entrance and threw dappled shade over the first half of the brass nameplate. I wondered if Mr. Delgado would make someone come and cut them down. I was pretty sure the whole point of naming it after himself was so that people could see it.

"This is it," I said.

I pulled on the large metal handle, but the front doors of the Delgado-Learner Building were locked. I stepped back and tilted my head up, scanning the building for signs of life. I should have known it wouldn't be that easy.

"What do we do now?" Kevin asked.

"Come on. There has to be another way to get in."

I led Kevin around the side of the building. The campus was full of students, but no one seemed too concerned with us. Maybe a lot of professors brought their kids to campus. Or maybe they thought we were geniuses getting an early start on our college degrees.

The windows along the side of the building were high and thin. They'd been designed to let in light, not distract the students inside with a nice view. Even someone as tall as my dad would have a hard time looking inside.

"Here, give me a boost."

"This is the real reason you brought me, isn't it?" Kevin got down on all fours, and I stood on his back so I could reach the window. The grass underneath him had just been laid. You could see the edges of each turf square where they hadn't grown together yet.

"Just try to hold still." I stuck my nose against the glass and looked inside.

The room was empty. Counters lined the walls, but there was nothing on them except for a fine layer of construction dust. Plastic sheeting hung down from the ceiling and off the walls, floating like ghosts in the hot, sticky air.

"It's not this one."

We checked three more windows and struck out each time. Kevin's knees got filthier and filthier, and so did his mood.

"Come on," I said.

"How about you let me climb on *your* back?"

"I don't think so."

"Fine, but the new bike you get me better be awesome," Kevin grumbled, and got down on the ground in front of the last window on the left of the building.

"I think this is it," I said.

Instead of an empty construction site, this room actually looked like a lab. There was still plastic hanging all over the place, but someone had tried to pin it to the walls so that it didn't get in the way. The shelves that lined the walls were full of equipment, the same equipment I'd seen in Dr. Learner's lab at Delgado Industries.

"Do you see him?"

"No." I held up my phone and took a picture of the room before I jumped off Kevin's back. "But he's been here."

"How can you tell?" Kevin stood up and tried to rub the grass stains off his knees.

"Well, for one thing, there are a lot of the same machines that I saw in Dr. Learner's lab."

"So? I bet lots of scientists use that stuff."

"Maybe, but do lots of scientists leave about fifty cups of coffee all over their lab?"

I held up the phone so Kevin could see the photo. It wasn't nearly as bad as Dr. Learner's apartment, but Kevin recognized the signature mess. It was hard to miss.

"And there's something else. Do you see that?" I zoomed in on the corner of one of the counters.

Kevin leaned over the phone. "It looks like a jewelry box. My mom keeps her pearls in something like that."

"It is a jewelry box. There was one just like it in Dr. Learner's office. Do you know what was in it?"

I paused for dramatic effect and then stopped myself. Della must have been rubbing off on me.

"There were diamonds. Ten of them."

Kevin looked at the phone, then at me, then at the window, like we could break into the lab and grab them.

"Dr. Learner found a way to use diamonds to make his lasers bend light. He's got to be one of the only people using them. This has to be where he's hiding. We just need to wait outside the front of the building and catch him when he comes back."

Kevin grinned. "You mean like a stakeout? Cool."

"You're starting to sound like Sammy." I laughed.

"Shut up."

We walked back around to the front of the building. The first drop of rain hit my nose. I looked up and groaned. So much for sitting on the bench. We pressed our backs up against the wall of the building under the shelter of the overhang. We'd stay dry as long as the wind didn't pick up.

I tried to call Mr. Delgado again, but it went straight to voice mail. They must be having some party if Andrew didn't even have the phone switched on.

"I don't get it," Kevin said. "Why is Dr. Learner hiding here? Why didn't he go farther away? I mean, this is his and Mr. Delgado's building, right?"

I had to agree with him. If Dr. Learner disappeared from Delgado Industries on purpose, the Delgado-Learner Science Building was a strange place to hide. It also seemed like the first place Mr. Delgado would have looked.

"Well," I said, "hopefully, Dr. Learner will show up soon and we can ask him ourselves."

(23

THE RAIN WENT from drizzle to downpour in a matter of minutes. I wasn't sure how likely it was that Dr. Learner would show up in this weather, but it wasn't like we could go anywhere without getting soaked. Kevin and I were stuck.

We'd been waiting for about fifteen minutes when Kevin broke the silence.

"So what are you going to do if we find Dr. Learner? I mean if he does show up?"

"I'm going to call Mr. Delgado and then I'm going to go get some lunch."

That wasn't completely true. What I really wanted was to ask Dr. Learner some questions about his research. Everyone I talked to seemed convinced that Dr. Learner had built an invisibility suit. It was starting to make me doubt myself. I hate doubting myself, but I didn't feel like explaining that to Kevin.

"You know that's not what I meant. What are you going to do with the rest of your summer?"

I leaned back against the building. The bricks were still warm from the morning sun, and they felt good against my shoulder blades. Water poured off the overhang above us. It was like we were standing behind a waterfall.

"I don't know," I said. "I haven't really thought about it. I'd planned to spend a quiet summer working on my math problems, but I guess it will depend on whether or not Della gets the part."

I shuddered and it had nothing to do with the rain. If Della didn't get the part after that *good luck* stunt I'd pulled this morning, I was in for a world of hurt. I wondered if the librarian would notice if I moved a sleeping bag into the stacks.

"You're going to spend the summer in the library doing math? I get that you're smart and you like that kind of thing, but come on, it's summer. Shouldn't you do something different? You know, something you can't do during the school year?"

"All right, what are *you* going to do?"

"Me? I'm gonna go camping with my dad."

"You? Camping?" I watched a watery figure run across the parking lot and disappear into a waiting car. It didn't look like Dr. Learner, but it was hard to tell through all the rain.

"Yes, me. It's fun. You should try it sometime."

I wrinkled my nose. Living in a tent with at least ten

mosquitoes and about a hundred other bugs you can't see did not sound like my idea of a good time. "No thanks."

Kevin sighed. "Suit yourself."

We stood side by side, watching the empty campus and waiting. All I could hear was the rain, drumming on the copper roof above us, spattering against the ground.

"My mom invited me to visit her in Italy," I said after a while, just to break the silence. At least, she had before my fight with Della.

"Really? That's awesome. The farthest away I've ever been is New York City for a Flyers game. You're going to go, right?"

"I don't know. It'll just be a lot of shopping and seeing shows. Mom and I don't really like doing the same kind of things."

"So? She's your mom—you're supposed to bug her until she does what you want."

I shrugged. I hadn't thought of it like that before. Maybe he had a point.

"Someone's coming." I pushed my shoulders off the wall and squinted into the rain. I could see a shape running up the path to the Delgado-Learner Building. It wasn't Dr. Learner; that much was obvious. He was too thin. But if he could get us into the building, I might be able to find a clue about where Dr. Learner was staying. And at least we'd be out of the rain.

He ran awkwardly, like he didn't do it very often. His backpack was pulled up over his head to protect him from the rain.

It made him look like a turtle. Kevin and I smiled at him as he got close. I needed him to let me into the building. But I was out of luck. He didn't have a key; he just pulled on the door and then looked embarrassed that it was locked.

"Is it supposed to be open?" I asked.

"No." He stepped back and looked at the brass nameplate, disappointed. "One of my classmates said he saw a professor going in the other day, so I thought I'd give it a try."

"A professor? What did he look like?"

"I don't know. I didn't see him. I just wanted to see the labs. They're supposed to be unbelievable."

My shoulders sank. I thought he might have seen Dr. Learner.

"If you're looking for one of the new science professors, you should check the university housing." He pointed behind us across the green. "They refurbished that old apartment block at the same time they built the new science building."

On the other side of the street was a plain brick building, three stories high. It was partially hidden from sight by a giant oak tree. It was right next to an electrical substation. I bet anyone living there could hear the wires humming all night long. But I wasn't worried about the living conditions.

"That's it. It must be." I turned to Kevin, then back to the student. "Thanks!"

"Sure," he said. He was confused, but I didn't think it would worry him for too long. To him we were just two kids looking for some random teacher. He didn't know we were about to crack the case of the disappearing scientist.

Kevin and I cut across the large green lawn next to the Delgado-Learner Building. Fat raindrops splashed on us and on the grass around us too quickly to count, but I didn't care. I hardly noticed that I was already soaked. I just ran.

"Where are we going?" Kevin yelled as he followed me.

"Don't you get it? None of the new professors will move in until fall when school starts. It's a great, big, empty building, right next to a state-of-the-art lab filled with Dr. Learner's equipment. It's the perfect place to hide."

I stopped at the side of the road and bent double, bracing my hands on my knees, and tried to catch my breath.

"Man, you need to work harder in PE." Kevin wasn't even winded.

"Not now," I gasped.

"I get what you're saying, but it doesn't seem right. I mean, wouldn't Mr. Delgado have checked there?"

"Maybe," I said. "But maybe not. Maybe it's so obvious that Mr. Delgado didn't even think to look here. Maybe Dr. Learner is hiding in plain sight. Or maybe I'm totally wrong and he isn't here at all. But we have to check it out."

I was so busy trying to convince Kevin that I almost didn't see the car until it was too late.

"Alice!" Kevin grabbed me by the back of my shirt and dragged me off the side of the road and into the bushes just as a bright, shining silver Mercedes drove by. I watched the back of the car disappear around the corner. They were driving in the direction of the Delgado-Learner Building parking lot.

"That was it, wasn't it?" Kevin said. "That was the car that's been following you. The guys who broke into your house."

"Yeah," I said, "that was them, all right. Come on, we need to hurry."

I didn't know how they'd found us. I hadn't seen the silver car all day, and I'd been looking. I started to get up, but Kevin stopped me again.

"What are you doing?" he said.

"Don't you get it? If they're here, it *must* mean we're on the right track. We need to get to that building first. If Dr. Learner is in there, we need to warn him. And if he's gone, we need to get the clues first so that Chronos can't follow us."

"Alice, those are the guys who broke into your house. They aren't just going to let you take him away. Even if you find him, what are you going to do?"

He was right. I didn't have a car, and Dad and Mr. Delgado weren't answering their phones. I should have let Sammy give me his number. I was sure he'd pick up. Then I remembered.

I reached into my bag and started pulling out papers and pens. All of the junk that I should have thrown away but never did.

"There!" I pulled out the card Officer Ross gave me. My fingers shook so hard it took me three tries to punch in the number. She answered after the second ring.

"Officer Ross? This is Alice Jones. You came to my house yesterday after someone broke in."

"Yes, I remember. Did something happen?"

"I saw that car that was following me again."

"Where are you now?" Officer Ross asked. I could hear one of her earrings click against the phone, tapping as she scribbled down the details.

"I'm at the University of Pennsylvania. They're going to the new Delgado-Learner Building."

"Are you safe? Did they see you?"

Kevin pressed closer, trying to listen, and I turned away before responding. "I'm OK; I'm on the side of the road. I don't think they saw me."

"That's good. Now listen, I want you to stay out of sight. We're on our way. Call me if anything happens."

I said that I would and hung up the phone.

I looked at Kevin. "There. Are you happy? Now let's go." I got up and tried to cross the road.

"Wait." Kevin yanked me back into the bushes. "What are you doing?"

"What do you want me to do, just sit here in the rain? If Dr. Learner is in there, we need to warn him. Besides, we'll be safer inside. There are doors in there. Doors with locks."

Kevin didn't look convinced.

"Please," I said. "Just trust me."

Kevin stared at me, and I stared right back. Maybe it was just a hunch, but I had to find out for sure.

"Fine, I'll go. But only because you'll need me if you get into trouble. And if we see those guys again, we run, understand?"

I nodded.

Kevin shook his head like he couldn't believe he was doing this. I didn't give him a chance to change his mind.

I checked the road carefully. The silver Mercedes had driven away from the apartments toward the Delgado-Learner Building. Hopefully, no one would tell them about the staff housing, and Kevin and I would get Dr. Learner out of the building without running into them. We sprinted across the street. I held my breath until we reached the leafy cover on the other side.

Someone had used a telephone book to prop open the door to the apartment lobby. I took it out as we stepped inside and let the door close behind us. The lock clicking shut sounded as sweet as a bell.

"This way." I pointed at the stairs. We'd have to check all of the rooms one by one. Dr. Learner wasn't going to hang a name tag under his doorbell.

I took the stairs two at a time. Two times eleven. Twenty-two steps. Kevin was right behind me. My legs felt like molten lead by the time I got to the top, but there was no time to rest.

"You check that side, I'll get this side." I had to admit it was nice to have someone to divide the work with.

I knocked on the first door. No answer. It didn't look like it had even been opened before. I knelt down to look closer. The door handles were still wrapped in protective plastic to keep the brass from getting scuffed. I didn't bother knocking on the rest, I just ran down the hall until I got to the door that had been unwrapped. Apartment 213.

"I found it," I said, and waved Kevin over.

"How can you tell?"

"It's the only one that doesn't still have plastic over the handle."

I knocked on the door. For a moment, there was silence. And then I heard footsteps. I knew I was right. The door opened.

"Hello, Dr. Learner," I said. "We've been looking for you."

(24

DR. LEARNER STOOD IN the doorway and blinked at us. He had a tablet in one hand and a stack of papers as big as a dictionary tucked under his arm. His hair was even wilder than it had been in the photos.

"I'm busy," he said.

I managed to wedge my foot between the door and the frame before it closed completely. "You don't understand, Dr. Learner. We're here to bring you home."

He opened the door again and peered out.

"Did Samuel send you?"

I was confused for a moment, then I realized he must have meant Mr. Delgado.

"Yes. Mr. Delgado asked me to find you. My name is Alice. This is Kevin."

Dr. Learner didn't move. He just stared at me like he was trying to remember something.

"We're friends of Sammy's from school. He's really worried about you."

Dr. Learner thought about it for a moment, then he let go of the door and walked back into the apartment. Kevin raised his eyebrows at me, but I didn't have any answers. I just shrugged my shoulders and followed Dr. Learner inside.

The apartment was smaller than the one at Drake Towers, but a lot nicer. The front door opened into a small hallway that led to the living room. A comfortable-looking couch and chairs took up the space to our left. The colors were all muted, except for a few accents. A red blanket here, a black table there. In the corner stood a small tree in the ugliest metal pot I'd ever seen. It was probably meant to be artistic, but I was more worried that the pot could slice open your leg if you weren't careful when you walked by.

Kevin checked the door to make sure it was locked and then slid the security chain into place. I guess he wasn't taking any chances.

Dr. Learner stood in the middle of the room, staring at us. It didn't make any sense. The way Sammy talked about him, I thought they were best friends. Maybe Sammy had exaggerated a little bit, but I'd seen the pictures of them together. I was sure Dr. Learner would be sorry he'd made Sammy worry, but he didn't seem to care at all. He hadn't even reacted when I'd said Sammy's name.

"Mr. Delgado will be on his way soon." I hoped Andrew had given him the message by now. I took out my phone. The signal kept cutting in and out. The substation outside the apartment building must have been creating interference. I tried the phone mounted on the apartment wall, but it hadn't been connected yet.

"You don't understand," Dr. Learner said. "I haven't found it yet. I still need more time."

Dr. Learner was pacing in the space between the glass coffee table and the couch. He had a look on his face like someone trying to describe a smell, like he knew what he wanted to say but couldn't find the right words. When I looked closely, I saw the carpet beneath his feet was worn. I wondered just how much of the last few days Dr. Learner had spent walking back and forth in that small line.

"Uh, Alice?" Kevin moved behind me and spoke into my ear. "Are you sure this is the right guy? He seems a little off."

"It's Dr. Learner," I whispered. "He looks just like his picture. But you're right, something is definitely going on here."

Outside I heard the faint keening of police sirens. They were still a ways off, but getting closer. It must be Officer Ross. All we had to do was sit tight until she picked up the men in the silver Mercedes. Then the three of us could walk out of here and this whole mess would be over. It also meant I didn't have much time to get Dr. Learner to spill the beans about how he'd managed to disappear from his office, and figure out the truth behind his invisibility research.

"OK, Dr. Learner. Let's start packing up these papers." I reached for a stack of notebooks on top of the coffee table, and Dr. Learner lost it.

"Don't," he shouted and shoved me, hard. He was strong for an old man, and I stumbled a few steps before I caught my balance.

"Whoa. It's OK." Kevin stepped between me and Dr. Learner. "It's OK. Calm down. She didn't mean anything; she was just trying to help you clean up."

Dr. Learner looked at me like I was some kind of wild animal. I held up my hands.

"I'm the only one who knows what order they go in," he said. He had the good grace to look a little embarrassed, but not much.

"OK, she won't touch them again."

Kevin looked at me, and I backed up a few more steps. Maybe Dr. Learner had been working a little too hard on his new invention.

Kevin waited a moment and then slowly stepped back from the couch until he was next to me.

"Are you OK?"

"I'm fine. But I'm not sure about him."

Dr. Learner was growing more and more agitated. Every third step he'd stop, riffle furiously through his notes, and then jot something down on his tablet. I didn't know what he was doing, but it looked like his life depended on it.

Suddenly, Dr. Learner stopped pacing. "I need to go back. It must still be there." He held up his tablet like he'd made a discovery, but I was pretty sure what he really wanted was to get away from us. Or at least to get away from me.

"Whoa, wait a second there," I said. I couldn't let Dr. Learner go outside until I was sure the men from Chronos were gone. He held his tablet close to his chest and looked at me suspiciously.

I turned to Kevin. "Keep him here. I'm going to find a signal and try calling Mr. Delgado again. He's Dr. Learner's friend. He might know how to deal with him."

Kevin nodded. He moved the red blanket off the couch and made room for Dr. Learner to sit down. I could hear him talking softly, asking Dr. Learner about his work, while I walked around the small apartment looking for a signal.

I got one bar in the hall closet, zero on the fire escape, and three standing on a chair in the kitchenette. I could have had all the bars in the world for all the difference it made. Mr. Delgado wasn't picking up. I climbed down from the chair.

Then I climbed up again and tried Officer Ross. She didn't answer either. I hoped it was because she was too busy arresting the jerks who broke into my house.

I thought about calling Dad, but he was going to be pretty angry and I didn't have time to deal with that right now. I needed to finish what I'd started and focus on getting Dr. Learner out of here safely. I sent Mr. Delgado a text telling him where we'd found Dr. Learner, and hoped he would check his phone sooner rather than later.

"Alice, bring me a glass of water," Kevin called from the other room.

The kitchenette was small, about a yard across, so it didn't take me long to find the glasses. They were in the second cupboard I opened, along with a row of pill bottles. They must have been the ones that were missing from Dr. Learner's real apartment. All of them were empty except for one. I turned it on its side so I could read the label. *Zelcore*. It didn't mean anything to me, but I'm not a doctor. I snapped a photo of the bottle and grabbed a glass.

Kevin had managed to calm down Dr. Learner. All of that practice sweet-talking himself out of trouble had finally come in handy.

"Here." I handed him the glass of water, then I sat down across from them. "Dr. Learner, we need to wait here until Mr. Delgado comes to get us. Do you understand?"

He looked at me, like he was seeing me clearly for the first time. His brown eyes were full of sadness. "I understand. It's OK. It was probably too late anyway. I just wanted to . . ." His voice trailed off. He scrolled through his tablet. If I twisted my neck to the side, I could just make out the pages and pages of complex equations racing across the screen. Dr. Learner frowned at the numbers and symbols as if he was trying to find one small mistake hiding in his calculations. "If I could just see it one more time . . ."

"See what one more time, Dr. Learner?"

He didn't respond, just scanned the equations again.

"Dr. Learner? What are you looking for? Does it have to do with the invisibility suit?" I tried not to let the frustration creep into my voice. "Why did you disappear from your office? And how did you do it?"

But Dr. Learner didn't answer me. He sipped his water and got lost in his own thoughts. I clenched my jaw and took a breath. I knew all I was supposed to do was find Dr. Learner. Mr. Delgado didn't even think I'd get this far, but it wasn't enough for me. I wanted answers.

I was about to ask him again when there was a knock on the door.

"Do you think it's the police?" Kevin asked.

I shook my head. "No, I told them to go to the science building."

"Maybe it's Mr. Delgado?"

"That or the men from Chronos R & D." I put my fingers to my lips and crept toward the door. My shoes didn't make a sound on the soft carpet.

I kept close to the wall so whoever was on the other side of the door couldn't see my shadow. The lock was new and the chain looked strong, so if it was the men from Chronos, we'd probably be safe. That felt about as comforting as a hug from a cold fish. I leaned diagonally across the small entranceway, bracing my arm on the opposite wall, and peered through the spyhole. It was Andrew. I almost slipped over, I was so relieved. Mr. Delgado must have gotten my message after all and sent his Personal Secretary to pick us all up.

I slid back the chain and opened the door.

"Am I glad to see you," I said. "Dr. Learner's here. He seems a little agitated. You might want to take him to see a doctor or something . . ." The words died in my mouth.

Standing behind Andrew were the two men from the silver Mercedes.

"I'm so sorry, Miss Jones," Andrew said. "I did mean to pass your message on to Mr. Delgado, but I'm afraid it must have slipped my mind."

(25

FOR A MOMENT I stood motionless in the doorway, my brain refusing to figure out why my body was panicking. Andrew was there to bring Dr. Learner back to Mr. Delgado. So why was he with the men from the Mercedes? And how had they found us? Then time skipped forward and it hit me like a train to the chest. Andrew and the men from the Mercedes had been working together the whole time. He must have had access to Mr. Delgado's phone, and I just texted him the address.

I tried to block the doorway. It was like trying to stop a tidal wave. The two men brushed past me without missing a step.

"Don't be dramatic, kid," Andrew said, dropping his android persona like it was a winter coat. "We're just going to take Dr. Learner and his research on a little drive. It's not like we're going to hurt him."

He held up a black overnight bag as if he was talking about

220

taking a camping trip. I looked around the apartment, searching for an escape route, but there was no way out. Andrew must have guessed I wanted to run. Before I could take even one step away, he grabbed my arm and twisted it behind my back.

"Kevin, run!" I shouted as Andrew marched me into the living room. If Kevin could find a way out, he could get help.

Kevin didn't listen. Instead of running away, he tried to tackle Andrew. But the men from the silver Mercedes got in the way. Kevin pushed one of them backward over the coffee table, then started toward the other one.

"Hey!" Andrew shouted. "Stay still or I'll break your girlfriend's arm." He pulled hard on my wrist, twisting it even farther behind my back. My shoulder screamed in pain and so did I.

Kevin stopped moving. It was the first time I'd ever seen him look truly frightened. My heart crashed against my ribs, and I couldn't tell if I was furious or terrified.

"That's better."

Dr. Learner sat still through the whole scene. The way he was staring into space made me wonder if he even knew what was happening.

"You." Andrew jerked his head toward one of his minions. "Take him into the bedroom and gather up his notes. Make sure you get everything. There should be a briefcase. And you"—he looked at the other man—"go grab me some chairs."

The man brought two chairs from the kitchen, and Andrew waved him off to go help his partner collect all of Dr. Learner's papers. For a moment, I thought Dr. Learner might save us all when they tried to mess with his research, but he didn't seem angry now, just scared.

Andrew knelt down next to his bag and pulled out a roll of duct tape.

"Now here's what's going to happen." Andrew patted his hand on the chair, inviting me to sit down. "Once we've gathered up all of Dr. Learner's research, we're going to take it, and Dr. Learner, on a trip. Our good friends at Chronos R & D are very interested in this little invisibility gadget he's been working on."

He motioned for Kevin to sit down in the chair behind me. With our backs to each other, I could feel how hard he was breathing.

"So you're a spy," I said, struggling to keep my voice from shaking. "You work for Chronos."

"I'm strictly freelance. Chronos just offered the best price."

"This is crazy. They'll never be able to use stolen research. Everyone will know." I kept trying to spin out the conversation, anything to keep him from taping me down.

"True," Andrew said. "But Chronos won't know it's stolen. At least, not until it's too late. You see, you're the only one who knows about all of this. And you won't be telling anyone anything. Not anytime soon." He waved the roll of tape playfully in front of my face. "As far as Chronos is concerned, I persuaded Dr. Learner to come of his own free will. I'll be out of the country before they have a chance to find out differently."

"They must be paying you a lot."

Behind me, Kevin twitched. I needed to think of a plan before he did something dangerous.

"Tons." Andrew moved my hands onto the armrests of the chair.

"Once I'm safe in another country, I'll call the police and let them know where to find you. It shouldn't be more than a day, so you'll be fine. See? I'm not such a bad guy, am I?"

"Wait!" I said, as he pulled the first strip of tape off the roll. It made a ripping sound.

"What?"

"You're gonna tie us up together, for more than twenty-four hours?" I asked.

"That's what I just said. I thought you were supposed to be smart."

I dropped my eyes and did my best to look embarrassed instead of angry. "Will you let me use the bathroom first?"

Andrew burst out laughing. It was a sharp, cruel laugh full of the enjoyment of other people's suffering.

"Sure, sweetheart, I understand. I wouldn't want to wet myself in front of someone I liked either."

I blushed for real, but kept my mouth shut. I needed him to keep laughing at me for this to work. Andrew grabbed me by the elbow and steered me toward the bathroom.

I looked at Kevin and opened my eyes wide. I hoped he'd catch the signal.

Then I took a deep breath and threw my head back with all of my strength. It hit the bottom of Andrew's chin with a satisfying crack. Andrew staggered slightly. Kevin didn't miss a beat. He leaped out of his chair onto Andrew's back, wrapping his arms around Andrew's neck and locking his legs around Andrew's knees.

"Get out of here!" Kevin shouted at me. I scrambled away from them on my hands and knees. I knew I didn't have more than a few seconds before the two men from the silver Mercedes came back and grabbed me. So instead of heading for the door, I crawled toward Andrew's getaway bag, and I stuffed my phone down to the very bottom, underneath a pile of papers and clothes.

I turned around to help Kevin, but it was already too late. Andrew had him pinned to the floor, his knee on the back of Kevin's neck. The other two men grabbed me by the arms and sat me back down in the chair. One of them held me there, while the other helped Andrew get Kevin into the other one. They taped Kevin up first.

"You won't get away with this, you know," I said to the man holding me down. "The police will catch you."

He just sneered at me.

"And give my sister her earrings back."

"Can I tape up her mouth?" he said over my shoulder.

Andrew came around to my side of the chairs. "What, is she getting to you? Just go get the papers together. I'll finish up here."

Andrew knelt down in front of me. I took a good look at the split lip I'd given him with the back of my head and smiled. Andrew smiled right back at me, and then he taped my right arm to the chair.

"It was a nice try," he said. He taped my left arm down too. "And I don't blame you for trying. In fact, I respect you. But I'm afraid you lost your bathroom privileges."

He checked my arms to make sure they were secure, then he bent and taped my ankles to the chair legs. Finally, he took the roll of tape and wound it around our chests, taping us together, back to back.

Kevin and I sat in silence while Andrew and his men did a final sweep of the apartment, making sure they had every last piece of Dr. Learner's research.

"Well, that looks like everything. I guess it's time to get this show on the road. I'll just take your phones, and then I'll be on my way. Would you like to tell me where they are, or would you like me to search you?" He smiled at us like this was a normal conversation.

"I don't have a phone," I said. My heart was pounding so hard I could feel it all the way into my fingertips.

"Now, Alice, I know that's not true. You called me on one, remember?" He pulled out his phone and showed me my number. "See?"

"I must have dropped it on my way here."

Andrew sighed. "Oh, Alice. I like you. You remind me of me, when I was your age. But I don't have time for games."

He pressed my number and my heart sank. I hadn't had time to turn my phone to silent.

I waited, adrenaline turning my nerves electric and raw. But there was no sound. Andrew frowned at his phone. He held it up and walked around the room. "Wow," he said. "There is really no signal here. I guess I don't need to worry about you calling for help after all."

He put his phone back in his pocket and snapped his fingers.

"Time to go, boys." Andrew held the door open for the two men from the silver Mercedes. They led Dr. Learner out of the room. He looked like a lost child at the supermarket, but that didn't bother Andrew at all.

"You kids be good now," he said with a salesman's smile, and slammed the door behind him.

(26

THIS IS WHY I said we should wait in the bushes," Kevin said. "Why didn't you run when you had the chance? You could have gone and gotten help."

"It would have been too late. Besides, I've got a plan. I snuck my phone into that jerk's bag. Can you stop jolting around? You're making the tape tighter."

"Well, excuse me. I've never been duct-taped to a chair before. And you *gave* him your phone? How is that a plan?"

"It's got GPS on it. We just need to get out of here, and then we can have the police track him down."

"You are unbelievable."

"Look, I'm sorry I got you into this, but right now the only thing we can do is work together and get out of here. Or do you want to wait for the twenty-four hours until Andrew calls someone to untie us? If he calls someone at all."

Kevin thought for a moment. I couldn't believe he needed to pause. Dr. Learner had looked like a lost puppy when those men had led him away. I didn't know what was wrong with him, but I knew going anywhere with Andrew and his flunkies was not going to help.

I could see the blue lights of the police across the street. They lit up the ceiling like flashes of lightning. Officer Ross was still out there, probably trying to get into the Delgado-Learner Building. But she wouldn't stick around forever. We needed to get out of there, fast.

"Kevin, I need you to help me."

"Fine," he said. Finally. "But I'm going to yell at you more later. Now, what do you want me to do?"

I took a breath and tried to calm down. I needed to think clearly.

"First we need to get out of these chairs. I don't think we can break the tape."

I looked around the room for something sharp. There. In the corner.

"We need to get over there. Next to that tree."

Taped together, the chairs were heavy. It took us almost ten minutes of grunting and shuffling to scoot across the three feet of carpet between us and the wall.

"Will you stop counting? You're driving me crazy." Kevin stopped pushing for a moment, and I realized he'd been doing most of the work. My toes scrabbled to find purchase and got nowhere.

"Sorry. Bad habit." My shirt was starting to stick to my back, and the duct tape around my chest was making it hard to breathe. "Can you keep going?"

I felt Kevin nod his head.

We shuffled in silence.

When we finally got to the corner, it took us another two minutes to scoot backward enough so that the edge of the metal plant pot pressed against my wrist. I started to push my arm back and forth, sawing away at the silver tape.

"I never thought I'd appreciate modern art," Kevin said.

I counted, in my head this time, as I sawed. At fifty-seven the duct tape was starting to fray. At eighty-six it snapped. My arm flew out, crashing into the pot. The sharp metal sliced through my skin. Blood dripped down from the gash in my arm, but I didn't care. I was free.

"Are you OK?" Kevin tried to turn around, and the tape pulled tight against my chest.

"I'm fine. Just give me a second." I used my free hand to unwind the tape on my other wrist. "Lean back as far as you can. I'm going to try to wiggle out of the chair."

Kevin pushed himself into the back of the chair, and I slipped down in my seat, pulling the tape off my shirt and away from my body. The edge of the seat scraped against my spine as I slid free. I pulled the tape off my ankles and went to help Kevin.

"Your arm!"

"It's nothing. Sit still."

I'd gotten his left arm free when the sirens blared once and then stopped. The flashing lights stopped too. Officer Ross was leaving.

"Wait here," I said. I ran across the room and peered out of the window. Dr. Learner's fire-escape balcony faced the Delgado-Learner Building. I could see police cars in the parking lot across the street.

"Hey," I shouted, opening the sliding door and waving my arms above my head. But I was too far away. The sound of falling rain swallowed my voice.

"What are you doing?" Kevin asked as I ran past him and grabbed the blanket off of the couch. I didn't answer, I just dashed back onto the fire escape, waving the bright red cloth like I was looking to fight a bull.

The cars were moving now, out of the parking lot and onto the road. I'd only have one chance to catch their attention as they drove past. I wiped the rain out of my eyes with the back of my hand, and then dried my palms against my shorts. I put one foot up on the lowest bar of the railing and hoisted myself up, leaning over the side of the balcony so that I could hold the red blanket over the edge. The worn treads of my shoes slipped worryingly against the metal.

"Are you crazy?" Kevin said. "Get down. Just come untie me so we can get out of here and call for help."

"There isn't time. Once Andrew gets his money from Chronos, he'll leave the country. Then they'll never be able to catch him. And what will happen to Dr. Learner?"

I climbed another rung. My shins pressed against the top of the railing. I leaned a bit farther out, holding the side of the ladder that led to the balcony above me. The blanket was so wet it felt like lead. The police cars were coming around the bend now. All I could think about were word problems. Two police cars traveling at thirty miles an hour. They'd only be able to see me for about fifteen seconds before they drove out of sight. I leaned out as far as I could and waved, yelling at the top of my lungs, trying to get their attention.

For once in this whole rotten case, luck was on my side.

The first police car braked, fishtailing on the wet road. The other car swerved to the side. I saw the lights go back on and the car door open.

"Up here," I shouted. My throat was raw. "We need help!"

I turned back to Kevin. He'd gotten his other hand free and was working on his feet. "They stopped. See. I told you this would work."

I should have climbed down before I started to gloat.

Maybe it was the relief, maybe I just couldn't hold on anymore, but my fingers slipped on the wet metal ladder rung. The weight of the soaking red blanket in my other hand tipped me forward, and I pivoted on my shins over the edge of the balcony and arced a perfect circle into the air.

I fell slowly. I had plenty of time to imagine all of the *I told you so*s Kevin would come up with once he stopped screaming. I could hear the police officers yelling too. A raindrop hit my cheek and seemed to push me toward the ground faster. I'd forgotten about the ground. I let go of the red blanket and watched the wind whisk it away.

I hit hard. The air rushed out of my lungs. I could feel the gentle tap of rain on my skin and hear the footsteps splashing toward me from the road. The police swarmed, asking questions I didn't have the energy to answer.

I managed to squeak out "apartment 213" and then I closed my eyes.

My dad was going to kill me.

(27

I OPENED MY eyes expecting to see clouds, but instead I saw white, square industrial tiles. The kind you get in dentist offices, or hospitals.

"Alice?" It was my father.

I could hear him moving away from me and opening a door, but I couldn't turn my head to see what he was doing. Someone had taped it to the table between two orange foam blocks. I groaned. Not more tape.

"She's awake," Dad called into the space beyond the door. Then he came back and stood next to the bed.

"Hi, Dad." My tongue felt two sizes too big for my mouth.

I could feel him squeezing my hand gently. "I thought I told you to leave the Delgado business alone. What were you thinking?" Dad's voice was a mixture of anger and relief. It didn't take a genius to figure out that I was going to be grounded for the rest of the summer.

The room started to fill with doctors and nurses, all poking me in different places. I felt like some sort of science experiment. Everyone was testing me for something. I counted three different nurses checking my pulse. Or maybe it was just one nurse checking my pulse three times. It was hard to tell when all I could see was the ceiling.

"Sorry," I said. "I really didn't think it would be dangerous. But I found Dr. Learner."

Dr. Learner. I managed to get my head an inch off the bed before the tape snapped it back.

"Can you take this off?" I asked one of the white coats. He didn't respond.

"I need to talk to Officer Ross. She needs to find my phone. Tell Mr. Delgado Andrew is a spy."

"Calm down, Alice." Dad leaned over me and put his hand on my forehead. He looked even worse than when I'd seen him that morning. "Kevin told the police everything. They tracked your phone and picked up Andrew and those other men going north on I-95. Dr. Learner was there too. You did it, sweetie. I'm proud of you, but promise me you'll never do anything like this again. OK?"

Dr. Learner was safe. The police had Andrew and the two men from the silver Mercedes. I was so relieved I forgot the tape and tried to nod.

"Don't worry, Dad," I said, grimacing. "I won't."

Dad squeezed my hand tight and bent forward to kiss me on the forehead.

"I'll bet you get the OK to write that exposé now, though," I said.

"I already got it. A two-page Sunday spread." He couldn't keep the smile out of his voice. "The editor wants me to write up your story too. You'll make it an exclusive, right?"

"Anything for you, Dad." I laughed. It was good to have my normal reporter-dad back.

One group of white coats was replaced by another. Dad went to fill out some forms, and I was left staring at the ceiling. I'd counted the tiles above me three times when one of the white coats came in and took off the tape. It was the best moment of my day.

I sat up slowly. Every inch of my back was sore, but nothing felt broken. I could wiggle all of my fingers and toes. I was testing out my neck, turning it from side to side, when I realized who was there. It was Della.

She was standing in the corner of the room, in the small triangle of space that would be behind the door if anyone opened it, clutching a thick stack of papers to her chest. It looked like a manuscript.

"Did you get the part?" I managed to croak.

Della stared at me, one eyebrow raised in artful disbelief.

"You idiot," she said. Then she rushed across the room and threw her arms around me. "I was so worried."

"Ouch, Della." I winced. "Careful, I just fell off a fire escape."

She hugged me a bit tighter and then let go, holding me by the shoulders and looking at me from arm's length. I could sort of see her taking a mental picture, so she could use this later when she needed to play the role of someone visiting the sick. I smiled. That was my sister, all right.

"I'm sorry we fought," I said.

"Me too." Della leaned on the side of the bed, half sitting, half standing. "I got so crazy about the audition. I was horrible to you and to Dad. I'm really sorry."

"It's OK." Even when she was being the world's biggest diva, Della was still my sister. "I tried to get your earrings back. But I was kind of taped to a chair."

"Alice, it's OK."

"But I bet you'll get them back soon. Dad said Officer Ross caught the men who broke into our house."

"Alice, I said it's OK. I didn't need them."

She stared at me, waiting for a response. When I didn't answer soon enough, Della made a show of sighing and rolling her eyes.

"I got the part."

She plunked the pile of papers she'd been holding triumphantly onto my lap. It was a script for *Annie*.

"You did?"

236

"Yes."

"That's amazing," I said, relief flooding my veins. "I was worried you wouldn't get it after I told you 'good luck' this morning."

Della glared at me, and then smiled again.

"It was OK—I kind of deserved it. Besides, you said it outside the theater, so I just had to spit on the street and swear three times before I went inside. Dad practically turned blue when he heard me. I didn't have the heart to tell him I learned it from Mom."

I laughed.

"And speaking of Mom," Della said. "She's worried about you."

I groaned, but Della showed no mercy.

"She made me promise to get you to call as soon as you woke up."

"But it's the middle of the night over there," I tried.

"I promised. As soon as you woke up."

Della took out her phone and handed it to me. Then she waited. I sighed. I was going to have to talk to Mom at some point. I guessed there was no time like the present. I pressed the call button and listened to it ringing.

"Della?" Mom picked up before the first ring had even finished. Her voice sounded too close to be coming from Italy. "Is there news? How is she?"

"Hi, Mom," I said. "It's me."

"Oh, Alice! I thought you were your sister. How are you? Are you hurt? What on earth did you think you were doing? You're just a girl—you shouldn't be out chasing criminals."

I probably could have put the phone down and had a full set of X-rays taken and she never would have noticed I was gone. But instead of disappearing, I interrupted her.

"I'm OK, Mom. Really."

Mom went quiet. I could tell she was trying not to cry. Della got her dramatic genes from Mom's side of the family.

"Mom, I'm honestly fine. Don't worry."

"Don't worry?" Mom snorted. I could practically hear her shaking her head from all the way across the Atlantic. "You just wait until you have a daughter. Then you'll understand."

I didn't have anything to say to that. I never did.

"Well, I'm just glad that you're all right. And that you aren't hurt. Will they let you out of the hospital soon?"

"I don't know," I said. "I think so."

"Did Della tell you I want you girls to come out and stay with me for a week or two at the end of the summer?"

"She did."

"Well, what do you think? Doesn't it sound like fun? Florence is so beautiful; I just know you'll both love it. It'll be good for you to get away for a while." Mom paused hopefully.

"Yeah," I said slowly. "Italy sounds like fun."

"Oh, honey, I'm so excited. I've got so many plans. There are so many places I want to take you and your sister. Wait till you see the theater I'm working in. Just breathtaking. And the stores here . . . Oh, I'm just so excited. The three of us are going to have such fun."

My heart sank. Shopping and shows it was, then. Or was it? I took a deep breath; it couldn't hurt to ask.

"It sounds nice, Mom. But do you think maybe I could pick out some things for us to do too? You know, more my kind of things?"

"Oh. Of course, honey. Whatever you like. I'll get the plane tickets, and you make a list of all the things you want to see."

"OK." I couldn't believe it. All this time trying to make Mom happy doing what she wanted to do, and she didn't bat an eyelid when I asked for something different. Kevin would crack up.

"Well, I'll let you get some sleep now. You call me as soon as you're home. I love you, honey."

"I love you too, Mom."

I hung up and handed the phone back to Della.

"So we're going to Italy," she said.

"It looks like it. And Mom says I get to pick some of our outings."

Della's falling face was a masterpiece of mock horror.

"Nice try," I said. "Prepare yourself for an education."

"How about this? I'll do my best to have a good time doing whatever it is you like to do, and you don't complain when we do what I like to do."

"That sounds like a deal."

We even shook hands to make it official.

(28

I SPENT THE rest of the evening being wheeled in and out of rooms, getting every inch of my body checked for damage. Apparently, Mr. Delgado was footing the bill, and he told them to spare no expense. They seemed to be taking him seriously. In fact, I think they may have invented some new tests just for me. By the time it was dark, I'd had more scans than I cared to count. And that is a lot of scans.

There was nothing much wrong with me. The doctor said that I had a mild concussion and some bruised ribs, so they'd have to keep me in for a few days for observation. But it wasn't anything serious. I wondered how much "observation" cost Mr. Delgado per hour. But from where I stood, a hospital bed beat another night on the couch.

When visiting hours were over, Dad didn't want to go home.

He kept insisting the nurses bring him some pillows and he would make himself comfortable on the floor.

"How can I leave you? Something might happen. You might need me in the middle of the night."

It was like being a three-year-old again. Not that I could get upset with him, not after everything I'd done. But sleeping on the hospital-room floor was going too far. Della stood waiting in the corner, holding her script and Dad's coat.

"Dad, she's fine."

"If I need anything, I'll press the buzzer for the nurse. I'm Mr. Delgado's personal guest. I bet a whole team will come running."

Dad didn't move.

"What about the Sunday spread? Don't you want to get started on that?"

Still nothing.

Della pushed herself off the wall and took Dad by the arm.

"Come on, Dad. There's a lot of stuff we need to do to get the house ready for Alice to come home."

Dad gave a startled snort and turned to look at my sister. After that, she had him in the palm of her hand.

"Think about it," she said. "We need to go shopping and make sure there's food, and maybe some new math books for Alice to read while she's resting or some DVDs to watch."

Dad looked horrified that he hadn't thought of it himself.

"And I was thinking." I could tell Della was going to hit him hard with her encore request. "Maybe you should move your computer up to your bedroom."

"Move my computer?"

"And your desk. Alice and I are getting a little old to be sharing a room."

"But you two always share when you come to visit. I thought you liked it."

"Well, it's fine for a weekend or so, but no one should have to sleep on an air bed for more than a week. And now that I've got a starring role, I need my own space." Della winked at me. "It's part of my process."

Dad looked at Della, then at me, then at Della again.

"So you see, there's a lot to do at home. We'll be able to help Alice more by letting her get a good night's sleep here while we go home and get things ready for her."

Dad nodded thoughtfully. My sister was a magician.

"You're absolutely right," he said. "Are you sure you'll be OK by yourself, Alice?"

"I'm sure, Dad. I'll be fine."

"All right. I'll be back to visit first thing in the morning. I love you, sweetie." He kissed me on the forehead.

Della pushed Dad quickly out of the room before he could change his mind. She turned once she got him into the hallway and gave me one last wink.

I mouthed the words *Thank you.*

Della smiled and nodded her head. A small bow to mark the end of a perfect performance. Then the door swung shut, and I was alone at last.

After Dad and Della left, I lay flat on the bed and stared back up at the ceiling. It was a lot earlier than I usually went to sleep, but it had been a very long day. I closed my eyes and tried to relax. Dr. Learner was safe, Andrew was in custody, and all was right with the world.

It shouldn't have taken me more than a minute to fall asleep, but for some reason my brain wouldn't stop whirring. *Sure,* it seemed to say, *you found Dr. Learner, but you didn't solve the equation, not really. Show your work, Alice. How did Dr. Learner get out of his office? And why? Is there an invisibility suit? And if there is, where the heck is it?*

I opened my eyes and stared at the ceiling. I told myself not to think about it. I counted the ceiling tiles in groups of ones, twos, and threes, but it was no use. I needed to know the truth. I sat myself up and pulled my bag off the bedside table and onto my lap. One of the police officers must have brought it to the hospital with me.

I pulled out my Goldbach's Conjecture folder and flipped to the back.

They were gone.

All my notes and the copy I'd made of the Delgado file were gone. Dad must have taken them out while I was unconscious.

I put the folder back in my bag and dropped the bag on the floor. I guess I couldn't blame him. I was just surprised he found it.

Maybe after all of the fuss had died down, I could convince him to give it back, or maybe I could talk to Dr. Learner and he'd tell me how he pulled it off. Although I'd rather figure it out myself. Either way, I needed to know. Or I might never get a decent night's sleep again.

I was just getting comfortable when the door banged open and Kevin Jordan wheeled into my room. He had a vase full of flowers on his lap. Every time he moved, it looked like water was going to spill all over him.

I propped myself up in bed. I didn't even mind the interruption. It wasn't like I was getting to sleep anyway.

"Hey," he said. "You're finally out of all those tests. I like your outfit, by the way."

I glanced down at my blue hospital gown.

"Yeah." I rolled my eyes. "I like yours too."

I looked at Kevin sitting in the wheelchair, his left leg strapped into an Aircast.

"Wait, what happened to you? Don't tell me you jumped after me."

"No. I tried to run after you when you fell out the window with my ankle still taped to the chair. It went *crunch*."

I winced. But it didn't seem to bother him that much, since he just kept right on talking.

"Man, Mr. Delgado is loaded, isn't he? My dad would have asked them to slap on a cast and call it a day. Delgado's got me staying overnight so the physiotherapist can assess me in the morning."

"He feels guilty we got hurt looking for Dr. Learner."

Kevin snorted as he wheeled himself over to the bed. I had to agree. Mr. Delgado didn't seem like the kind of guy who felt guilty about much of anything. It was more likely that he was worried how it would look if he didn't take care of us. After all, we were great publicity.

"Here," he said, handing me the vase. "My mom brought them for me, but they stink. I thought you might want them."

"Thanks, I think." I put the flowers on the bedside table. They were nice, but I was surprised Kevin's mom had gotten him something so girly.

"You scared the crap out of me when you went over that railing. I seriously thought I was going to have a heart attack. You must be made of titanium or something."

"It wasn't that far down, and I think the rain softened up the ground."

"Whatever. It was pretty cool. I can't believe we solved the mystery. Do you think we'll be in the paper?"

"I don't know. Probably." When your dad's a reporter, being in the paper doesn't seem that exciting, but I didn't want to rain on Kevin's parade.

"What's the matter? Why aren't you more excited?"

"I don't know. I was hoping Dr. Learner would tell me how he did it. Maybe I can get Della to bring me my file . . ."

"Don't tell me you're still obsessing about how that guy got out of his office? It doesn't matter. You found him. End of story. Case closed." Kevin slapped his palms together. Then he looked at me and grinned. "The more important question is, what are you going to do with your half of the reward money?"

"Excuse me?"

"You heard me. I got taped to a chair. I deserve half."

I looked at Kevin. His angel face smirked back at me. For the first time I kind of understood the charm. "Fine," I said. "We'll split it. But you're buying your own bike."

(29

I WAS EATING breakfast when Mr. Delgado and Sammy came to visit. Dad had gone out to find me some real coffee, and Della was sitting in the green chair by the window learning her lines. *Annie* rehearsals started next week, and she wanted to be word perfect. I had a feeling I'd be reprising my role as Miss Hannigan before the day was over. But after the night before, I owed her.

"And how is my little detective this morning?" Mr. Delgado reached out and patted my head like I was a dog that had just performed a trick. "Receiving the best care, I hope? The director of the hospital is a personal friend of mine. I made him promise to keep a special eye on you."

Mr. Delgado handed me a large bunch of roses. They took up my whole lap and half of my face. Della looked at me and rolled her eyes. Then she took the flowers and went to find something to put them in. I watched her walk out the door and wished I could escape too, but I was stuck in bed, and Mr. Delgado was waiting for an answer.

"Everyone's been very nice to me."

"I should think so. This hospital owes me a lot of favors." He rocked back on his heels, practically beaming. Sammy was beaming too.

"I told you she'd do it, didn't I, Dad? Alice is amazing."

I could feel my face turning red. How long did it take to find a vase for some flowers?

"She is indeed," Mr. Delgado said. "Although I wish you'd called me instead of rushing out there all by yourself. If something serious had happened to you . . ."

It would have been very bad press, I finished his sentence in my head.

"She did try to call you, Dad, remember? She left a message with Andrew."

Sammy should have kept quiet. At the mention of his traitorous Personal Secretary, Mr. Delgado stopped beaming and started scowling.

"Ah, yes. Andrew." He said the name like it was poison. "I can't believe Chronos had the nerve to infiltrate my lab. Bribe my Personal Secretary. And kidnap our top scientist. Well, they'll be hearing from my lawyers, make no mistake about that."

He was on a roll, but something he said didn't make sense.

"But they didn't kidnap Dr. Learner," I said.

Mr. Delgado stopped blustering and stared at me, hard. "What are you talking about? Of course they did. The police found them together in a car."

My head started to pound. Dad needed to hurry up with that coffee. I reached up to rub my temples and tried to gather my thoughts. "Well, maybe they kidnapped him from the apartment. But until I called Andrew, they didn't know where he was, so they couldn't have kidnapped him the first time."

Mr. Delgado's eyes narrowed, and he took a step toward my bed. For a moment, I thought he might actually bite me. Even Sammy looked a little nervous. But he didn't bite. Mr. Delgado reached out his hand and put it to my forehead, then smiled.

"You need to stop thinking so hard. Stop worrying. You'll get wrinkles."

The door opened, and Dad and Della came in before I could respond, Dad carrying a cup of coffee from the store across the street, Della carrying the roses in a large plastic jug. She put them on the bedside table next to the ones Kevin had brought the night before. She didn't say anything, but she didn't need to. I could have seen her smirking from the other side of the hospital. She made sure to put Kevin's flowers closer to the bed so they wouldn't be hidden by the roses.

"Mr. Jones." Mr. Delgado shook hands with my father. "I spoke to the doctors. They agree there's no reason for Alice to stay in the hospital any longer. But they'll want her to take it easy at home for a while. Someone will come to speak with you soon."

Dad smiled weakly. I wondered if he'd slept at all or if he'd stayed up all night working on his exposé.

"I just want to take her home," Dad said. And then his reporter instincts kicked in. "I don't suppose you have a moment to talk right now? I'd love to get a comment from you on a story I'm doing on one of your competitors." Dad pulled his notebook out of his back pocket. It made me smile to see him back on his game.

"Of course," Mr. Delgado said. I could practically see him rubbing his hands together, getting ready to tell Dad all about Chronos's evil ways. "Actually, I've called another press conference for tomorrow, just a small one. I want to let everyone know that Adrian is safe. And, of course, I want to present Alice with her reward check." He turned to me and smiled. "I understand you're going to share it?"

"I had some help." I didn't look at Sammy. I knew he'd hit me with the puppy eyes, and then I'd feel guilty I wasn't splitting the money with him too. Although I don't think Sammy cared about the money. He only wanted to be my partner. But no matter how bad I felt about saying no, that was still the answer. Sammy was a nice kid, but his hero worship was exhausting. If I was going to have a partner, it needed to be someone who could stand up to me and tell me when I was starting to act a little crazy.

"Well, tell your helper to come with you." He turned back to my dad. "But for now, Mr. Jones, I'm happy to give you whatever information you like. Let me buy you a drink, and I'll tell you everything you need to know about Chronos Research and Development."

My dad followed Mr. Delgado out of the room, notebook and pencil in hand, leaving Sammy standing at my bedside looking sheepish.

"I *knew* you'd do it." He beamed and handed me a small blue gift bag tied up with an elaborate mess of curling ribbons. "I know you don't need it anymore, but I thought you might like it anyway." Sammy leaned a little closer. "I did my best to wash it. Sorry if it still smells."

I peeked into the bag and shut it quickly. But all I needed was one glance to know exactly what was inside. It was an L-shaped piece of metal. The bracket from the security camera. Sammy had found his rainbow frog. And from his comment about the smell, it had been in the trash, just like Kevin had guessed.

"Thanks, Sammy," I said.

I was pretty sure Mr. Delgado wouldn't be too happy if he knew Sammy was giving me more clues. I understood. Things had worked out great for him. He had a new contract, his top scientist was back, and his competition looked like they were about to get a one-way ticket up the river. He didn't want me rocking the boat. But there were still so many things that didn't add up.

I looked down at the little metal clip like maybe it had the answers. But if it did, it wasn't talking.

"Sammy?" I asked without looking up. "Do you think Chronos kidnapped Dr. Learner?"

Sammy danced from foot to foot. I could feel him jiggling the bed. "I don't know," he said, shrugging his shoulders. "But it doesn't matter anymore. Dr. Learner is back." Sammy sounded happy, but he sounded something else too. He sounded relieved.

"Sammy, what did you think I was going to find in Dr. Learner's apartment? Dr. Learner said something similar. He said he needed to go back. That it must still be there."

Sammy didn't answer. Or he *couldn't* answer. He just licked his lips and stood there.

"Was he talking about the invisibility suit?"

"No. I don't know. It doesn't matter." Sammy tried to back away naturally, but he didn't do a great job. "Dad's right, you worry too much. Dr. Learner is back. Everything is fine now." Sammy reached the wall with a bump. "I need to go. I'll see you tomorrow at the press conference. Dad said I could have my picture in the paper. It'll be great!"

And with that, he opened the door and fled.

Even though the doctors said I could leave, we had to wait three hours before someone finally came and signed the discharge papers. They gave me a prescription for anti-nausea pills I didn't need, but we went to the hospital pharmacy anyway.

Dad went to gather up my flowers and Get Well Soon cards while Della and I waited in line at the pharmacy. Della said she was staying with me to make sure I didn't faint, but I was pretty sure she just wanted a break from Dad's story fever.

"The typing, Alice. I couldn't sleep a wink. How can he make so much noise typing?"

"I like Dad's typing. I think it's soothing."

"Well, then I want the downstairs bedroom. You can have your old room back."

"Sounds good to me." I handed my prescription to the pharmacist. "And thanks. About the separate rooms, I mean."

"I don't know what you're talking about. I need my own space. Didn't you hear? It's part of my process." Della smirked beautifully.

Behind the counter were three giant towers of shelves. Each shelf spun around so the pharmacist didn't have to move. He found the pills that matched my prescription and began counting them out into a small orange bottle.

It was just like the pill bottles I'd found in Dr. Learner's apartment.

"Have you ever heard of Zelcore?" I asked.

He frowned. "No."

Della pinched the back of my arm. "Why are you asking him about that?"

I ignored her and tried again.

"Really? Maybe I'm pronouncing it wrong." I pictured the letters on the bottle in Dr. Learner's apartment and sounded out the word again. He still didn't know what I was talking about, so I spelled it.

The pharmacist shook his head. "I'm afraid I can't help you." He put my pill bottle in a white paper bag and handed it to me across the counter. "You could try looking it up online. It might be an experimental medication. We don't get any drugs here until they've been fully tested and approved."

"Thanks. I'll try that."

"Alice," Della said as we walked away from the counter, "why were you asking him about some mystery drug?"

"I saw a bottle in Dr. Learner's place. I thought it might be a clue. Maybe I got the spelling wrong. I took a picture, but the police still have my phone."

"Oh my God, Alice. You just can't let it go, can you? You and Dad are as bad as each other."

Dad was waiting for us by the exit. Kevin sat next to him, trying to balance his wheelchair on its back wheels.

"Hey, Numbers. Check it out. The physiotherapist gave me a lollipop."

"How old are you?"

"I got extras. You want one?"

He held out a handful of lollipops. Della and I both helped ourselves.

"Is there anyone you can't sweet-talk?" I asked.

Kevin grinned. "Nope."

"Kevin was going to be stuck here until his mother finishes work, so I offered to bring him home and feed him. That OK with you?" Dad asked, taking a lemon lollipop for himself.

I shrugged. Why not? Another hour with Kevin wasn't going to kill me, was it?

I regretted it when I realized driving home with Kevin meant sitting in the backseat with his broken foot on my lap and listening to Della giggle about it from up front. I think Dad was giggling too; he was just better at hiding it. It was the only time in my life I felt like Dad's driving was too slow.

(30

AFTER WE ATE lunch, Dad grabbed his water bottle, told Della and Kevin to keep me out of trouble, and headed upstairs to put the final touches on his exposé before the Sunday paper's deadline. I sighed. It was going to be a long time before Dad let me out unattended.

Della waited until the door to Dad's bedroom/office slammed. Then she turned her million-dollar eyes on Kevin. "How would you like to help a star prepare for her Philadelphia debut?"

Even Kevin Jordan couldn't say no to my sister.

Della had already made copies of the pages she wanted us to practice with her. She handed them out with a professional air and led the way to the couch. Della sat on it like it was a throne. Kevin propped his leg up on the arm. That didn't leave a lot of space, so I took the floor.

It should have been easy. But no matter how much I tried to concentrate, all I could think about was Dr. Learner's impossible disappearing act.

The room was sealed. I'd been over the whole office, and I was certain there was no way in or out besides the one door. And the security camera showed that Dr. Learner went in that way, but he never came back out.

$$(\text{one exit}) + (\text{security camera footage}) +$$
$$(\text{disappearing man}) = x$$

I'd gone over the equation again and again, but I wasn't any closer to solving it than when I started. Della nudged me with her toe, and I read my next line. I could feel my eyes glazing over before I got to the end of it.

If I could just find the right combination of variables and move them into the right place, everything would be clear.

$$(\text{one exit}) + (\text{disappearing man}) =$$
$$x - (\text{security camera footage})$$

Maybe Dr. Learner had figured out some way to fake the security camera footage. He was a scientist who worked with lasers and light. Maybe he figured out a way to fool the camera or hack into the security system.

Or maybe it went more like this:

$$(\text{one exit}) + (\text{security camera footage}) =$$
$$x - (\text{disappearing man})$$

Dr. Learner used his invisibility suit to disappear, just like Graham Davidson said. Maybe he knew Chronos was after him, and he wanted to escape. Although that didn't explain why he didn't tell Mr. Delgado. It didn't explain why he acted so strangely when we found him either.

"Alice? Alice!" Della shouted, and I jumped in my seat. "It's your line."

"Sorry, I was thinking." I shook myself back into the room. Kevin gave me a look, begging me to save him. I guess reading Daddy Warbucks wasn't his idea of a great night in.

"Where were we?"

Della crossed her arms and tipped her head to the side. "It's no use, is it?" she said. Then she knelt down next to the couch. "I'm only doing this because you won't be any use to me until you get that stupid mystery out of your system."

She reached under the couch and pulled out a plastic folder filled with papers. I caught a glimpse of the first page, and my heart skipped a beat. It was the Delgado file.

"Here," she said. I reached out to take it, but Della snapped it back. "Don't let Dad catch you."

"Cross my heart and hope to die." There was no way I'd let him know I was still looking into the case. But there was also no way I'd be able to rest until I knew how Dr. Learner had gotten out of that room.

"You have to help me run my lines all week."

I nodded so hard my neck hurt.

"And"—Della held the folder just out of reach of my fingers—"I want roses on opening night."

"Yes, yes, anything you want. Now give it to me."

I snatched the folder and shook out the pages. Everything was still there, even the mirror from Mr. Delgado's office. Della must have taken it all out of my Goldbach's folder before Dad had a chance to search it. She was amazing.

"Pass me that bag, the blue one," I said.

Kevin handed me Sammy's gift bag, and I pulled out the metal frame. The mirror slotted into the empty space perfectly.

"What is that?" Kevin asked.

"It was hooked to the security camera outside Dr. Learner's office. It's the key to the trick, I know it. I just haven't figured out how."

"Let me see it." Della put out her hand, and I gave it to her. She held the frame up to her face and peered into the mirror, pushing her hair back behind her ear.

"It's like a magic box."

"A what?"

"It's an old stage trick."

Della launched into a tale about some off-Broadway production of *The Wizard of Oz* that she was in. About how the theater didn't have a trapdoor for the Wicked Witch of the West to use, so they'd rigged up a mirror onstage to make it look like she appeared out of thin air.

I closed my eyes and tried to remember. Hadn't Mr. Delgado said something about magic before? No, it was a photo. He and Dr. Learner had been in a magic act together.

"It took them forever to get the angle right," Della rambled on. "On opening night, it looked like there were two Wicked Witches of the West. It was a disaster."

That was it.

I shuffled through the folder until I found the floor plan of Delgado Industries. I lined up the mirror on the page, centering it over the security camera. I couldn't get an accurate angle with the paper spread over the carpet, but it was close enough. The mirror changed the angle of the camera. I remembered the first time we went to the lab and Andrew was complaining about the nameplates. But they'd needed to take those off in order to make all the doors look the same. The security camera had been filming the sealed door next to Dr. Learner's door the whole time.

I sat back on my heels and took a deep breath. It was like coming up for air after spending too long at the bottom of the pool. Everyone else had been so convinced the suit was real, I'd almost started to believe it myself. It was a relief to finally have proof that my suspicions were right all along. There was no high-tech invisibility suit; it was all done with smoke and mirrors.

Well, not with smoke. But definitely with a mirror.

Someone had stood out of view of the security camera and waited for Dr. Learner to go into his office. Once he was inside, they carefully slid the mirror into the bracket that was fastened to the camera. With the right calculations, the mirror would change the view of the camera, creating a blind spot in the security footage. Once the mirror was in place, Dr. Learner could walk out of his office and no one would ever know. Then all they needed to do was wait until Dr. Learner was behind the camera, take out the mirror, and *Poof!* Dr. Learner had vanished without a trace.

And now that I knew how the trick was done, I knew who was behind it.

The mirror might have gotten Dr. Learner out of his office unseen, but it couldn't get him out of the rest of the building. At least not out the front. The only way Dr. Learner could have exited the building was through Mr. Delgado's office. And the only person who had a key to Mr. Delgado's office was Mr. Delgado.

He'd set up the whole thing. I just didn't know why.

"Della, can I use your phone? The police still have mine."

I typed in *Zelcore*. There was one result. A paper posted by the University of Pennsylvania's medical school.

Zelcore is a new class of cholinesterase inhibitor cur-rently undergoing phase two clinical testing at the

University of Pennsylvania Hospital. Zelcore has shown promising results in delaying the worsening of symptoms of Alzheimer's disease from between nine to eighteen months. Preliminary results from the phase one and two studies indicate that Zelcore will be significantly more effective than existing medications.

I finally knew what Dr. Learner was running away from. He was running away from himself. I shuddered. I couldn't imagine anything worse than having a disease that would slowly erode my mind. It explained why Mr. Delgado wanted him out of the way too. No one is going to sign a multimillion-dollar contract with a company whose top scientist is losing his ability to invent.

All the pieces fit into place, the equation balanced, and I had my answer. I just had no idea what I was supposed to do next.

(31

THE MORNING OF the press conference, Della did her best to make me camera-ready. She vetoed my usual summer uniform of cargo shorts and a T-shirt and marched me to the closet to pick out a dress.

"You've got to be joking," I said, looking at the row of flounces and frills hanging in front of me.

"Alice, you're going to be on TV. Either you pick one, or I'll pick one for you." Della grabbed the corner of an especially pink and sparkly number and waved it at me menacingly.

"All right, all right," I said. "But I'm not wearing heels."

I pulled out the hangers and picked the least ruffly dress I could find. It was light green and made out of soft fabric that bounced on the hanger. I didn't like it, but at least I'd be able to breathe.

When Della finally let me downstairs, I'd been painted and

polished until I could barely recognize my own face. Dad's jaw hit the floor when he saw me.

"You look so grown-up," he said. And he actually started crying.

"Keep it together, Dad." The powder Della had used was making my face itch. But that wasn't the only reason I felt like snapping. I'd spent the whole night trying to decide what to say to Mr. Delgado. I still hadn't figured it out.

Dad's Plymouth looked as out of place as ever as we pulled up to the Delgado Mansion. Kevin and his family were already there, waiting near the front steps. Kevin was wearing a suit.

"Listen," Kevin said when he saw the face I was making. "If you don't say anything, I won't say anything."

I took a quick look down at the dress Della had loaned me. "Deal."

As we walked up the steps, Sammy came out to meet us. He was wearing a suit too, but on him it looked natural. He probably got his first suit when he turned one. I smiled at him, and then I remembered I still needed to talk to Mr. Delgado, and I felt my smile turn to stone. My fingers tightened on the strap of my messenger bag. Della had tried to make me carry one of her purses, but I'd put my foot down. I needed something big enough to hold all my notes.

"Come on in, it's a little hectic." Sammy held the door open for us.

The large white entrance hall was full of people standing in small groups and looking slightly lost. This time I counted three different TV crews. There was even a group from the national news. I guessed Mr. Delgado and I had different definitions of the word *small*. Bruno and Brutus were there too, holding back the reporters as I, Dad, Della, Kevin, and Kevin's mom and dad walked through the room.

"This is so great!" Sammy said. "Here, follow me." He led us into the study, past the corralled reporters and their questions. When the heavy wooden door shut behind us, the sudden silence made my ears ring.

"This is very nice, Sammy. Did you help set all of this up?" Dad asked.

Sammy could barely contain himself. "No, Dad's got a new PR company. He hired them after Andrew was, um, fired. And a new personal secretary, she's really nice. I like her."

It looked like Mr. Delgado had big plans for Delgado Industries. I wondered how long ago he'd hired that PR company, but it didn't really matter. I already knew everything I needed to know.

"Does anyone want a drink? Or some snacks? I can go and get them. Dad said I needed to be a good host."

"Wait, Sammy." I grabbed his sleeve before he bolted. "Where's your dad? I need to talk to him."

"He's through there." Sammy pointed toward the door

behind the large desk at the back of the room. The same door Mr. Delgado had walked through the first time I laid eyes on him. I told my family I'd be right back. Dad made a move like he wanted to follow me, but I waved him back. I had to talk to Mr. Delgado alone. He'd been behind the whole thing, but I wanted to give him a chance to come clean on his own. I owed Sammy that much.

"Mr. Delgado?" I knocked on the door and let myself into a small office. It must have been where Mr. Delgado did his business when he wasn't trying to impress people.

"Ah, Alice, the star of our show. Come in, come in." He had a circle of paper towels tucked into his collar and a dark-blue cape of thin fabric over his front, the kind you wear when you get a haircut. A young woman with bright pink hair was brushing powder across his large flat face.

"Well, well, well. You clean up very nicely when you make an effort, don't you? Although, you might want just a touch more powder. Those lights the TV crews brought can be very unforgiving. And no one wants to look bad on TV. Have a seat. Sylvia can touch you up once she's finished with me."

Sylvia smiled at me, but I shook my head. "I'm fine, thanks."

"Suit yourself." Mr. Delgado shrugged. Sylvia held up a mirror for Mr. Delgado to check her handiwork. He nodded thoughtfully. "Maybe just a touch more off the brows. I don't want to look like an old man."

He leaned back and closed his eyes while Sylvia brushed his eyebrows with some sort of mini-comb, nipping off the ends with a pair of nail scissors. When he opened his eyes, he seemed surprised that I was still there. He seemed a little annoyed too, but I wouldn't want someone watching me get my eyebrows trimmed either.

"Was there something you wanted, Alice?" he asked absently while checking his eyebrows in the mirror again.

"We need to talk," I said. It seemed like the only way to start.

"What do you want to talk about?"

"We need to talk about Dr. Learner's invisibility suit."

Mr. Delgado smiled. He pulled off the cape and handed it to Sylvia.

"I can neither confirm nor deny the existence of any invisibility suit," he said. He had a laugh in his voice, like he was enjoying some kind of private joke. "Are you sure you don't want some more powder?"

I ignored the second question. "You don't need to confirm or deny anything, Mr. Delgado. I *know* there's no invisibility suit," I said. "I know you used a mirror to trick the security camera, and I know about Dr. Learner's medical condition."

He turned sharply in his seat and stared at me. Underneath all of his makeup, I could see his face going red. "Thank you, Sylvia," he said. "That will be all."

She took the hint and scooped all of her tools into her bag in one fell swoop, then ducked out of the side door.

Mr. Delgado didn't say anything right away. I think he was counting to ten. When he finished, he smiled at me. It looked just like all of his other smiles, but there was nothing behind it but teeth.

"It isn't nice to discuss private business in front of people who aren't involved."

"It isn't nice to do a lot of things." I gripped the strap of my bag a little tighter, holding on for dear life.

"I don't know what you think you know, but you couldn't be more wrong. Making false accusations can get you in a lot of trouble." He leaned forward in his chair, but he didn't get up.

"But I'm not making false accusations," I said. "You helped Dr. Learner disappear from his office and reported it to the world because you didn't want anyone to know he had Alzheimer's disease and that the invisibility suit research was a dead end. Especially not the government. They never would have signed that forty-million-dollar contract with your company if they knew the truth."

"What are you talking about? Adrian is one of my most brilliant scientists. Now that he's back, Delgado Industries will continue to—"

"I found his medication."

I couldn't tell if he was going to yell at me or laugh. He didn't do either. He put his hands over his face and started to cry.

Not real crying. He didn't want to ruin his makeup, but it was pretty convincing. Della would have been impressed.

"You don't understand at all." He took a deep breath and collected himself, then hit me with his big sorrowful eyes. He looked a lot like Sammy when he did that. "Everything I did, I only did to protect Adrian. You need to understand that.

"Six months ago, just after he finished the invisibility cube, Adrian began to behave strangely. I finally got him to see a doctor, and they told us what it was. Adrian was devastated." Mr. Delgado's voice cracked. He turned his head to one side and swallowed hard. I didn't say anything. After a moment, Mr. Delgado continued.

"Science is Adrian's life. He was terrified that it was all going to slip away from him. Can you imagine what it must be like for someone who's spent their whole life trying to push the boundaries of physics to know that they are slowly going to lose their mind? Adrian *is* his brain. He was always all about the science. And all I ever wanted to do was help him achieve his goals. When he won the Beakman Fellowship, people thought I was jealous. Everyone always thinks I'm jealous, but I never am. I just wanted to help Adrian change the world."

Mr. Delgado barely stopped long enough to catch a breath. He glanced at me out of the corner of his eye. I knew what he was doing. He was trying to make me feel bad. I hated to admit it, but it was working. He licked his lips and kept talking.

"Adrian's life's work was invisibility. All he wanted to do before he stopped being able to work was to leave something behind. I promised him that if he couldn't complete the invisibility work himself, I would dedicate Delgado Industries to finishing his work for him. I also promised him I wouldn't let Sammy find out about his illness. He didn't want anyone to know what was happening to him."

He smiled sadly and shook his head, every inch the loyal best friend and loving father. Maybe part of him believed that his story was true. Mr. Delgado was right about one thing: Sammy would be heartbroken. It almost made me wish I hadn't figured things out. For a minute, I thought about telling Mr. Delgado to forget the whole thing. And then I thought about waking up every morning and living with a lie. Sure, it was a nice, soft, comfortable lie, but it was a lie all the same. I just couldn't do it.

"No," I said.

"Excuse me?" Mr. Delgado sounded confused. I guess he didn't meet a lot of people who told him no. He looked at me like I was some kind of alien.

"It doesn't add up. There were lots of other ways you could have protected Dr. Learner and Sammy. You didn't need to stage it so it looked like the suit was working. You didn't need to trick the government into signing your contract. You did that for Delgado Industries. You didn't want to lose your big chance to be one of the top labs in the country, so you faked the whole thing."

"You be very careful, young lady. I never once said there was an invisibility suit. I can't help it if people jumped to conclusions. If they're disappointed, it's their own fault for not doing more research. Besides, now that we have the money, I'm sure we'll have a fully functioning suit in no time."

"I don't think they'll see it that way." I folded my arms.

Mr. Delgado's eyes narrowed. He stood up so suddenly I couldn't stop myself from flinching. In two giant steps, he was across the room and standing so close I couldn't get out of my chair.

"No, they won't. They won't see it any way at all. I don't know who you think you are, or what you're trying to pull with this little stunt, but it isn't cute."

He leaned forward and gripped the armrests of my chair. Underneath his powder he'd gone purple with rage, his nostrils flared slightly. I could feel the blood draining out of my fingers and toes, like it was running for safety. My brain knew he couldn't hurt me, not with a room full of reporters on the other side of the door. But my survival instinct was telling me to run.

I took a deep breath and told my knees to stop shaking. Mr. Delgado wasn't done yet.

"Now I'm going to tell you what you are going to do," he said. "You are going to go out there and smile nicely for the cameras. And you're going to shake my hand when I hand you your reward check. And when the reporters ask you questions, you are going to keep your mouth shut like a good little girl. I'm a very powerful man, and if you don't behave yourself I can make life very difficult for you. *And* your father. Do I make myself clear?"

I nodded. Mr. Delgado was as clear as crystal. He wanted me to be quiet, or else.

"Good."

Mr. Delgado stood up and straightened his collar. He'd forgotten about the paper towels and pulled them out angrily, letting them drop to the floor. He shook himself, the way a dog shakes off water, and suddenly he was Mr. Delgado the charming businessman again. He smiled at me and held open the door, motioning for me to go first.

I nodded politely. Mr. Delgado had made a mistake, but I didn't think he'd want me to tell him that. He'd asked me if I understood what he wanted. And I did. I understood perfectly. But that didn't mean I was going to give it to him.

I smiled my best, most obedient smile and then stepped through the door to face the music.

(32

MR. DELGADO HERDED ME to one of the chairs set up behind his desk. His study was full of reporters now. Their questions and cameras sounded like the percussion section of a jazz band. Kevin was already in his seat waiting for us. It looked like Sylvia had caught him after Mr. Delgado kicked her out of the room. He kept touching his forehead and then looking at his fingers to see if anything had rubbed off.

I didn't hear much of Mr. Delgado's speech; there was too much blood pounding in my ears. Time seemed to slow down with each heartbeat, and I had the chance to get a good look at every member of the audience one by one. The woman from the *Times* chewing the end of her pencil, the man from the *Independent* rolling his eyes at one of Mr. Delgado's jokes. The group of statues from the first press conference were back, looking pleased with themselves. They must have been the ones from the government who signed the contract with Delgado Industries. I squeezed my bag between my fingers, tracing the outline of the Delgado file. They weren't going to stay pleased for very long.

In the front row, Della stuck her fingers in the corners of her mouth and pushed her lips into a grin, telling me to smile. I wiped my palms against the sides of my dress and tried to ignore the feeling that the room was starting to spin.

Mr. Delgado's hand on my shoulder brought the world back into focus. I blinked and caught the end of what he was saying.

". . . and I have this brilliant little girl to thank for bringing Dr. Learner back to us." He smiled down at me like we were best friends, but I could see the threat behind his eyes and feel it in his too-tight fingertips.

I caught Dad's eye as I stood up. Everyone else looked like they were buying Mr. Delgado's story, but not my dad. He might have had to write a puff piece, but he'd never stopped digging for the real story. That was my dad all over. One man on a mission to find out the truth. I smiled for real this time and nodded slightly. Dad wiggled his eyebrows in anticipation. It felt like I was five years old all over again, staring out at all the parents and judges of the Little Miss Friendship pageant. Dad knew I was about to pull something then, and he knew it now.

Mr. Delgado kept right on talking. "And now, on behalf of

Delgado Industries, I am very happy to present this reward to Miss Jones."

A man from Mr. Delgado's bank stepped forward holding a large cardboard check, the kind you always see on TV. Mr. Delgado held out his hand, waiting for me to shake it. Flashbulbs popped and whirred as the photographers clicked away, and the reporters who weren't taking pictures tucked their notepads under their arms so they could applaud. I caught a glimpse of Sammy beaming from the front row, looking at me like I was some kind of hero.

For a moment, I hesitated. Would it really be so bad to let Mr. Delgado get away with it? No one got hurt, not really. Sure, Andrew and his goons would go to jail, but they deserved it. They broke into our house, kidnapped Dr. Learner, and taped me and Kevin to chairs. I looked at Mr. Delgado, and then at Sammy. It wasn't fair. I wanted to stick my head in the sand and leave it there until this whole mess went away.

But I couldn't. I'd solved the problem, and I couldn't hide the truth, even if it was just by keeping quiet. I knew what had really happened. Saying nothing was just as bad as telling a lie.

I took a deep breath and looked Mr. Delgado square in the eye.

"Sorry," I said softly. "I gave you a chance."

Then, before he had time to react, I turned to the members of the press and made my statement.

"I can't take this check. The whole thing was a scam. Mr. Delgado set it up himself to fool everyone into thinking Dr. Learner had finished the invisibility suit. He hasn't. There is no invisibility suit."

I tried to squeeze as many words as possible into one breath, because I knew as soon as Mr. Delgado realized what I was doing, he'd try to stop me.

And I was right.

I'd barely gotten the last word out of my mouth when I felt his hand close around my arm, his fingers digging into my flesh so hard they'd leave a mark.

He was trying hard to stay cool, but I didn't know if he'd keep it together. He looked like a bull getting ready to charge. I could almost see the steam coming out of his nostrils.

Mr. Delgado glared at me and opened his mouth. I jerked my head to the side, reminding him we had an audience. He turned his head and stared at them blankly. At least fifty members of the press stared back, waiting to see what he'd do next. I've never seen a room full of reporters so quiet in my life. Mr. Delgado swallowed. Hard. He let go of my arm, nervously smoothed his hand across his hair, and tried to paint the smile back on to his face. It came out a little crooked.

"Now, Alice, it isn't good to make jokes like that. People might think you're serious."

"I am serious." I turned back to the press. "And I can prove it." I pulled the Delgado file out of my bag and held it high over my head. Dad looked shocked that I had it, but I was pretty sure he'd let it slide. I was about to hand him the story of a lifetime.

The reporters couldn't keep quiet anymore, and the room erupted into questions. Mr. Delgado held up his hands for quiet, but no one was paying attention to him anymore. At the back of the room, the group from the government scowled as they got out their phones and started making important-sounding calls.

Mr. Delgado watched the room crumbling around him, and then he looked at me. The person who'd made it crumble. I don't know what I'd thought was going to happen. I hadn't planned that far ahead. I figured someone like Mr. Delgado would handle it pretty well.

But he didn't. He didn't handle it well at all. In fact, Mr. Delgado completely lost it.

He lunged forward, trying to grab the file out of my hand. I stepped sideways and ran to the other side of the space-age desk. I wanted to put something large and solid in between the two of us. I didn't like the look in Mr. Delgado's eyes one bit. I hoped that Mr. Delgado would remember where he was and get ahold of himself. But he didn't, or he couldn't.

He followed me around the desk, faster and faster. It was almost funny except I wasn't sure what would happen if he caught me. His eyes were bulging now, and no amount of makeup could hide the way his face twisted with rage.

"Stand still, you little brat!" he shouted. "Do you have any idea who I am? I'll ruin you. You and your whole pathetic family. And your friends. You'll have nothing. Now give me that file, you worthless little—"

I never found out what name he was going to call me. Mr. Delgado's high-polish shoes weren't meant for running. He tried to take the corner around the edge of his desk too quickly and wiped out spectacularly, taking half the contents of his desk onto the floor with him. The oversized check went down too, snapping with a loud crack.

I bent over with my hands on my knees and tried to catch my breath. Kevin was right, I did need to work harder in PE.

"You OK, sweetie?" Dad asked. He'd gotten out of his chair and stood next to me. I nodded. Della was there too. And she had her fighting face on.

Mr. Delgado's hand grabbed the top of the desk, and I tensed, ready to run again. He pulled himself onto his feet and brushed the dust from the front of his jacket, sniffed, and gave me the coldest stare he could muster. Then he reached up to smooth his hand over his hair, and froze.

Mr. Delgado's slick black hair had flipped open like the lid of a trash can, revealing the very smooth, very pale dome of his scalp. The room started to giggle. Mr. Delgado blushed deep red and hastily pushed his hair back into place.

"Stop laughing," he said. "And turn off those cameras. All of you. I do not give permission for any of you to use anything you filmed today." His voice rose to a shriek. He kept one hand glued to the top of his head, holding his hair in place. No one stopped laughing, and no one turned off their cameras either. News was news, and there was nothing Mr. Delgado could do about it.

"I said turn them off! Don't you know who I am?" He picked up the nameplate from his desk and waved it in the air. "I'm Samuel Delgado!" He raised the nameplate high over his head and then smashed it to the floor. "I'll sue you. And you. I'll sue all of you, for defamation of character and lost income! I'll have all of your papers shut down!" With every threat, Mr. Delgado picked up another object from his desk and threw it. And with every item he threw, he looked more ridiculous and the laughter in the room grew louder.

His eyes fell on a shell-shocked-looking woman standing at the back of the room. That must have been his new personal secretary. She looked like Andrew version 2.0.

"You!" he shouted at her. "What do you think I'm paying you for? Make them stop recording." Mr. Delgado's voice shook her, but it was too late for her to do anything now. Instead, she slipped out the back of the room. Mr. Delgado practically howled as the door shut behind her.

Mr. Delgado looked around the room wildly, like an animal caught in a trap, and with one last crazy effort he leaped into the audience, charging like a rhino toward the nearest cameraman. But he didn't make it.

The personal secretary reappeared just in time, with Bruno and Brutus right behind her. The two henchmen rushed across the room and caught Mr. Delgado in midair, and then dragged him kicking and screaming out of the room, leaving the rest of us in silence.

Dad came to his senses first. I saw him whisper something to Kevin's mom and she nodded, grabbing Kevin and his father by the arms and moving to the back of the room while Dad got everyone's attention. Kevin looked at me, confused, but I waved him on. This was their chance to escape without getting mobbed by the press.

"Hello, fellow reporters," Dad said. "Well, that was something, wasn't it?"

The room laughed appreciatively.

"Now, I know a lot of you, and a lot of you know me. And I know how much we all love a good story. *But* I'm afraid, even for a reporter, family comes first. So I'll be taking my two lovely girls home with me, and they won't be answering any questions."

He held up his hands before they could protest, and we all

edged toward the door. "Alice will release a statement about the case, along with all of her proof, after she speaks with the authorities. And, of course"—he grinned—"after she speaks to me." He grabbed my hand and Della's. "OK, girls," he said, "now we run."

We bolted out of the room through Mr. Delgado's antechamber. Dad shoved a chair in front of the door to buy us some more time, and then he led us into the white entrance hall and out the front door. Dad heaved it open, and we sprinted across the driveway. We were almost at the car when Sammy caught up with us.

"Alice!" he shouted. My heart sank.

I motioned for Dad and Della to get in the car as I ran across the gravel drive to meet him halfway. I didn't know how he'd beaten the reporters, but we didn't have much time before they caught up.

"Alice, why'd you do that?" he asked. He looked confused and hurt all at the same time. I felt awful.

"I'm sorry, Sammy. I gave your dad a chance to tell the truth, but he wouldn't do it. I didn't have a choice."

I couldn't tell if I was trying to convince him or myself.

"But he's not lying. There was an invisibility suit!" Sammy said. He grabbed my hand and started pulling me back toward the house. "You need to tell them you were wrong."

I pulled myself free and crossed my arms tight against my chest. "I'm not wrong, Sammy. There is no suit."

"There is!" he said, stamping his foot on the gravel driveway. "You have to believe me!"

I looked at the door over his shoulder. Behind me, Dad honked the horn.

"Sammy, if you're so sure there's a suit, where is it? If there's a suit, all your dad needs to do is get it out and prove me wrong."

Sammy mumbled something and looked down at his shoes like they were the most interesting things he'd seen all day.

"What?"

"I said he can't! I lost it!"

Dad honked the horn again. I held up my hand for him to be patient.

"I don't understand."

Sammy kept staring at his shoes. His shoulders heaved a few times, then he took a deep breath and started to explain.

"Dr. Learner was supposed to help me with my science project this year. But when I went to his apartment he wasn't there. I knew he was really busy, I just wanted to help . . ."

"What happened?"

"I tidied up for him, that's all. I just wanted to help. He was so busy and the apartment was such a mess. I just wanted to help."

"I get it, Sammy." All Sammy ever wanted to do was help.

"No, you don't. The next day he didn't come to work, and when I went to see him, he was searching his apartment. He was really angry. He kept saying he couldn't find it, or that someone stole it or hid it. Don't you see? I must have put the invisibility suit away somewhere when I was cleaning. Maybe I even threw it out. I took out so much trash."

And there it was. I knew Sammy had been hiding something from me, and now it all made sense. Sammy thought Dr. Learner's disappearance was all his fault. He thought he had lost the suit and made Dr. Learner run away. I shook my head. Poor Sammy. It must have been awful, especially with a dad like Mr. Delgado. No wonder Sammy was so desperate for me to find Dr. Learner. He thought if I found him, I'd find his research, and no one would ever know Sammy lost the suit. The problem was, Sammy was assuming the suit was real. And I knew it wasn't.

"Look, Sammy. Dr. Learner—" I stopped. Dr. Learner didn't want anyone to know he had Alzheimer's disease. But it didn't seem fair to let Sammy keep thinking Dr. Learner really finished the suit. Especially if Sammy was blaming himself for losing it. "Dr. Learner is sick. He never made a suit. He was just confused because you moved things around. You'd have known if you saw something as important as that. Besides, I was in his apartment; there wasn't any suit there. And if someone else found it, we'd know by now."

"But it's invisible! How are you supposed to find something you can't see?"

He stared at me so intently, I knew there was no arguing with him. And he did have a point. But an invisibility suit that was invisible all the time—that would be an awful design. It would be impossible not to lose it. No one in their right mind would invent a suit like that, would they? Sammy kept on talking.

"You were supposed to find him *and* the suit. You were supposed to make everything better, not get my dad in trouble."

The door to the Delgado Mansion opened and the crew from Channel 4 spilled out into the driveway, pointing in my direction. Dad honked the horn hard. I was out of time.

"I'm really sorry, Sammy. I really am. But I couldn't lie. I just couldn't."

I left Sammy standing in the middle of the driveway and sprinted back to the Plymouth. As I jumped into the car, I got one last glimpse of him, running past the reporters and back into his house. I knew I'd done the right thing, but that didn't stop me from feeling like the worst person on the face of the planet. Whoever said the truth will set you free should get hit by a bus. Dad slammed his foot on the accelerator before I closed the door. It swung open dangerously as he sped around the Delgados' circular drive, and then slammed shut on its own as we swerved the other way into traffic.

(33

WE DROVE HOME in silence. Dad didn't ask any questions, but I could hear him tapping his fingers against the steering wheel as he drove. I tipped my head back and just stared at the ceiling. The fabric above me was starting to pucker and loosen as the old glue gave up its fight with gravity. I knew how it felt—worn-out and saggy.

When we got to the house, I followed Dad up to his new bedroom-office and I told him everything.

I told him about finding the medicine in Dr. Learner's apartment and what it meant, and how Mr. Delgado had planned the whole thing and why. I told him how Mr. Delgado had threatened me, and how Sammy thought it was all his fault. I told him how Dr. Learner wanted to keep his disease a secret. And I told him how telling the truth would hurt just about everyone involved: not just Mr. Delgado, who deserved it, but the people who worked for him, and Dr. Learner too. Something sharp twisted in my middle as I remembered the look on Sammy's face when we drove away. He'd never forgive me. But if I'd kept Mr. Delgado's secret, if I'd lied . . . I fumbled for the right words like they held the solution.

Dad didn't say a thing. He didn't even move except to hand me a box of tissues. He just listened and looked sad.

"There must have been a way, right? A way to make everyone happy?"

Dad put his arm around my shoulders. "There's never a way to make everyone happy," he said. "But forget about everyone else. What will make *you* happy? Will you feel better if I kill the story?"

Dad's question was such a shock I stopped crying and just stared at him. There was no way Dad would pass up the scoop of the century just like that. He must have seen my disbelief.

"Look, sweetie," he said with a sigh, "I've been a reporter all of my life. Believe me, I know how hard telling the truth can be. Sometimes people get hurt, people who didn't do anything wrong. If you don't want to be a part of hurting Sammy, I understand. Everything you told me is off the record and I won't print a word of it."

I sniffed hard. It was tempting, but it was no use. I already knew what I had to do. I finished crying and wiped the snot off my face.

"Write it," I said.

"Are you sure?"

"The truth will come out." I took a deep, shuddery breath. "I'd rather it came from you."

"That's my girl." Dad put his hand on the back of my head, pulled me tight against his chest, and kissed the top of my hair. I sniffed a few more times, but I didn't cry. It hurt, but at least it was a clean kind of hurt. Not the gnawing pain of keeping a secret that's too big to hold on to.

Dad waited until I'd calmed down again before he started writing. At first I watched him type, then I just lay back on the bed and listened. The keys clattered so quickly and close together they sounded like rain, like my dad was typing a storm that would wash the whole world clean.

The story ran on the front page the next day. And a week after that, I saw Mr. Delgado on the news being arrested. Dad had tried to be sympathetic in his story, but facts were facts. Mr. Delgado had tricked the government into signing a contract. The government was not amused.

As they led Mr. Delgado away, he did his best to look dignified. His suit perfectly pressed, shoes gleaming, and all of his hair in the right place. But it wasn't much use. Someone had posted the footage online of him falling over his desk and coming up bald. It took less than an hour to go viral. The only thing people like to watch more than a man in a suit falling over is a man in a suit falling over and then having a massive temper tantrum about it. Even if Mr. Delgado didn't get convicted, no one would ever take him seriously again.

I tried to spot Sammy in the crowd, but he wasn't there. Later, Dad found out that he'd been sent to stay with an aunt in Arizona. Dad said she sounded nice and that Sammy seemed happy there. I hoped he was right. I wrote him a letter to say sorry, but I never heard back from him. Not that I blame the kid; I wouldn't want to talk to me either.

"It's not your fault, you know," Kevin said. He'd showed up the morning after Mr. Delgado's arrest, demanding that I help him finish the rest of his workbooks. Summer detention had started days ago, but I guessed he'd sweet-talked Principal Chase into giving him an extension. Maybe she saw the story Dad wrote about us and felt bad she hadn't believed him before.

"What are you talking about?"

"You. You're moping around like it's your fault Mr. Delgado got in trouble. It isn't. You didn't do anything wrong. They did. It wasn't your job to protect everyone." Kevin was on a roll now, his blond curls bouncing. I could just picture him holding a sword—an avenging angel indeed.

"Hey, don't laugh. I'm serious," he said. "You gave him a chance. He should have come clean on his own."

"That would have been nice."

It would have been even nicer if Mr. Delgado had come clean about Dr. Learner's condition from the start. If he hadn't planned the magic trick of the disappearing scientist and led us all on such a wild-goose chase, none of this mess would have happened.

"I'm sorry you didn't get the reward money," I added.

Kevin shrugged. "It's no big deal. It's not like I can ride a bike right now anyway." He wiggled his cast at me. "I just wish we'd found the suit."

"There was no suit." I rolled my eyes.

Kevin leaned back in his chair and crossed his hands behind his head. "I don't know. I mean, Sammy's a little strange, but what he said *could* be true. Maybe it was in Dr. Learner's apartment the whole time and we just couldn't see it."

I shuddered at the memory of Dr. Learner's filthy apartment. It was hard enough to find things that *weren't* invisible in all that mess, let alone something that was. The image of that one clean square of space next to Dr. Learner's bed flashed into my brain. I'd assumed that it was empty because someone had taken something away, but what if I was wrong? What if it hadn't been empty at all? Could the suit have been right there in front of me the whole time? For a moment I considered the possibility, and then logic kicked back in.

"No," I said. "It can't be true."

"Ah." Kevin grinned like the devil. He'd been waiting for that. "But you can't *prove* it isn't true, can you?"

I stared at him, mouth open. He was right. No matter what I believed, I couldn't prove he was wrong. Kevin tapped his pencil on the counter like he was playing the drums. I think he was enjoying himself.

"Don't you have a workbook to finish?" I asked. I was also pretty sure he was trying to annoy me so I'd stop moping about Sammy.

"Three more questions, ma'am." He gave me a quick salute and got back to work.

Despite what Kevin said, sometimes I still wondered if I'd done the right thing. Maybe if I'd kept my mouth shut, or asked Dad to write the story in a different way, I could have made everyone happy. I spent hours lying on the couch trying to figure out where I'd gone wrong. Trying to find the perfect solution.

Maybe that was why I liked math so much. An equation might be tough, but that nice, clean, correct answer on the page when you finally worked it out? That was beautiful.

I guess life just wasn't so easy. Telling the truth was as close to perfect as I could get.

Kevin finished the last problem and stretched back in satisfaction.

I reached across and took the worksheet so I could check his answers. I could feel him watching me while I worked.

"So, your sister's opening night is coming up?"

"She told you too?" I didn't look up.

"Are you going with anyone?"

"I'm going with my dad."

Kevin went quiet. I put down the workbook and stared at him.

"Wait, you want to come see *Annie* at the Walnut Street Theatre? You're joking."

Kevin's cherub cheeks turned bright pink. "I helped your sister rehearse. I think I should go see her perform."

I laughed. "OK, fine. I'll take you to see *Annie* if you promise to come to the Franklin Institute to see the M. C. Escher exhibit with me."

Kevin looked appalled. "Wait, I have to go see *Annie and* go to a museum?"

"Hey, you're the one who wants to go to the play." I folded my arms. *Take it or leave it, pal.*

"Fine, but you have to push my wheelchair."

We stared at each other so hard, I could almost feel sparks.

"All right, it's a deal."

I went back to checking the workbook. He'd actually done

a pretty good job. I wondered what Kevin would think if I asked him to help me prove Goldbach's Conjecture. The thought of him juggling all of those prime numbers was so funny it was almost worth a try.

What can I say? I like a challenge.

Acknowledgments

SPECIAL THANKS to the Kids from the Dark Side (Dave, Vila/Celeste, Geoff, and Deven) for pointing out the good, the bad, and the ugly, and helping me fill in those pesky plot holes. Thanks also to Lawrence and David for their feedback as early beta readers.

Thank you to my wonderful agent, Lindsey Fraser, for her encouragement and support as well as her editorial advice. A critique from Lindsey always makes me excited to write another draft!

I'd also like to thank the team at Chicken House. I was thrilled to work with them again, and though some of the faces may have changed, the spirit of joy and imagination and their love of great stories certainly hasn't! Thank you to Barry Cunningham, Rachel Leyshon, and Kesia Lupo, for helping me keep sight of the fantastical.

Finally, I'd like to thank my whole family for their love and support: to my dad for taking me to the Franklin Institute and teaching me that learning is fun; to my mom for always having a bookshelf full of mysteries; and to my husband, Chris, for being a *real* math expert and keeping me (and Alice) on the straight and narrow.

About the Author

SARAH RUBIN grew up splitting time between Philadelphia and an island off the coast of Maine. She spent most of her childhood playing dress-up, reading, and trying to get lost in the woods.

Sarah earned a BA in creative writing and history from Skidmore College in New York State, and after teaching dance and drama for a year, she moved to Winchester, England. She is the author of *Someday Dancer*.